Seadove

Seadove

Seadove

Seadove

The Gardener 中英對照

園丁集

泰戈爾最經典的詩集！

羅賓德拉納德·**泰戈爾** *Rabindranath Tagore*/著

徐翰林/譯

愛情和生命，永遠是泰戈爾的浪漫追求！

Who are you, reader, reading my poems an hundred years hence?

I cannot send you one single flower from this wealth of the spring, one single streak of gold from yonder clouds.

Open your doors and look abroad.

From your blossoming garden gather fragrant memories of the vanished flowers of an hundred years before.

In the joy of your heart may you feel the living joy that sang one spring morning, sending its glad voice across an hundred years.

你是誰，讀者，百年之後，讀著我的詩？

我無法從春天的財富裡為你送去一朵鮮花，從遠方的雲彩裡為你送去一縷金霞。

打開你的門，向四周看看。

從你的繁花盛開的花園中，採集百年之前消失的鮮花的芬芳記憶。

在你的內心的歡樂裡，願你感受吟唱春日清晨的鮮活喜悅，讓歡快的聲音穿越一百年的時光。

The Gardener

Who are you, reader, reading my poems an hundred years hence?
I cannot send you one single flower from this wealth of the spring, one
single streak of gold from yonder clouds.
Open your doors and look abroad.
From your blossoming garden gather fragrant memories of the vanished
flowers of an hundred years before.
In the joy of your heart may you feel the living joy that sang one spring
morning, sending its glad voice across an hundred years.

你是誰，讀者，百年之後，讀著我的詩？

我無法從春天的財富裡為你送去一朵鮮花，

從遠方的雲彩裡為你送去一縷金霞。

打開你的門，向四周看看。

從你的繁花盛開的花園中，

採集百年之前消失的鮮花的芬芳記憶。

在你的內心的歡樂裡，

願你感受吟唱春日清晨的鮮活喜悅，

讓歡快的聲音穿越一百年的時光。

1

僕人：女王啊，寬恕您的僕人吧！

女王：集會已經結束了，我的僕人都走了。這麼晚了，你來做什麼？

僕人：您與別人的事情結束了，就應該是我的時間。我過來問問，還剩下什麼事情要讓您最後的僕人去做。

女王：這麼晚了，你還期望做什麼呢？

僕人：讓我做您的花園的園丁吧！

女王：荒唐！

僕人：我會擱下我的其他事情。我會把我的劍與矛扔進塵土中。不要把我送到遙遠的宮廷；不要命令我作新的征討。就讓我做您的花園的園丁吧！

女王：你將會履行什麼職責呢？

僕人：侍侯您的閒暇時光。我會讓您在清晨散步的時候，隨時看到小路上芳草鮮嫩，您的腳每挪動一步，將會有鮮花甘願冒死來問候與讚揚您。我會讓您在七葉樹花枝間的鞦韆上搖盪，初升的月亮掙扎著穿過枝葉，親吻您的長裙。我會給您的床前燃著的燈盞裡注滿芳香的燈油，用檀香和番紅花膏塗成奇妙的圖案，裝飾您的腳凳。

女王：你想要什麼回報？

僕人：允許我捧著您的小拳頭，像捧著柔嫩的蓮花花蕾，把花鏈滑到您的手腕上；用無憂花的紅色花汁染紅您的腳底，親吻掉偶然間灑落在那裡的塵埃。

女王：你的請求被准許了，我的僕人，你將是我的花園的園丁。

$O\mathcal{N}E$

Servant: Have mercy upon your servant, my queen!

Queen: The assembly is over and my servants are all gone. Why do you come at this late hour?

Servant: When you have finished with others, that is my time. I come to ask what remains for your last servant to do.

Queen: What can you expect when it is too late?

Servant: Make me the gardener of your flower garden.

Queen: What folly is this?

Servant: I will give up my other work. I throw my swords and lances down in the dust. Do not send me to distant courts; do not bid me undertake new conquests. But make me the gardener of your flower garden.

Queen: What will your duties be?

Servant: The service of your idle days. I will keep fresh the grassy path where you walk in the morning, where your feet will be greeted with praise at every step by the flowers eager for death. I will swing you in a swing among the branches of the saptaparna, where the early evening moon will struggle to kiss your skirt through the leaves. I will replenish with scented oil the lamp that burns by your bedside, and decorate your footstool with sandal and saffron paste in wondrous designs.

Queen: What will you have for your reward?

Servant: To be allowed to hold your little fists like tender lotus-buds and slip flower chains over your wrists; to tinge the soles of your feet with the red juice of askoka petals and kiss away the speck of dust that may chance to linger there.

Queen: Your prayers are granted, my servant, your will be the gardener of my flower garden.

2

「啊，詩人，暮色就要降臨了，你的頭髮變白了。」

「在你的孤獨沉思中，是否聽到來世的消息？」

「是黑夜了，」詩人說，「我還在聆聽，因為可能有人在村子裡叫我，儘管很晚了。」

「我觀望著，是否有年輕漂泊的心相聚，是否有兩雙渴望的眼睛乞求著音樂來打破他們的沉靜，替他們道出心聲。」

「誰會在那裡編織他們火熱的情歌，如果我坐在生命的海岸，思索著死亡與來世？」

「夜初的星辰消隱了。」

「寂靜的河邊，殯葬堆中的火焰慢慢熄滅了。」

「疲憊的月光中，豺狼在廢棄的庭院中齊聲嗥叫。」

「如果某一個離家的流浪者，來這裡觀看夜色，垂首聆聽黑暗的低語，誰會在他的耳邊輕訴生命的意義，如果我關上門，試圖與世俗的羈絆隔絕？」

「我的頭髮變白了，只是一件小事。」

「我永遠像這個村子裡最年輕的人一樣年輕，最蒼老的人一樣蒼老。」

「有些人微笑了，甜蜜的，純真的；有些人的眼中，閃著狡黠的光。」

「有些人在白天揮灑著眼淚，有些人的眼淚隱藏在黑暗中。」

「他們都需要我，我沒有時間去思索來世。」

「我與每個人都同齡，我的頭髮變白了，又能怎麼樣？」

TWO

"AH, poet, the evening draws near; your hair is turning grey."

"Do you in your lonely musing hear the message of the hereafter?"

"It is evening," the poet said," and I am listening because some one may call from the village, late though it be."

"I watch if young straying hearts meet together, and two pairs of eager eyes beg for music to break their silence and speak for them."

"Who is there to weave their passionate songs, if I sit on the shore of life and contemplate death and the beyond?"

"The early evening star disappears."

"The glow of a funeral pyre slowly dies by the silent river."

"Jackals cry in chorus from the courtyard of the deserted house in the light of the worn-out moon."

"If some wanderer, leaving home, come here to watch the night and with bowed head listen to the murmur of the darkness, who is there to whisper the secrets of life into his ears if I shutting my doors, should try to free myself from mortal bonds?"

"It is a trifle that my hair is turning grey."

"I am ever as young or as old as the youngest and the oldest of this village.

"Some have smiles, sweet and simple, and some a sly twinkle in their eyes."

"Some have tears that well up in the daylight, and others tears that are hidden in the gloom."

"They all have need for me, and I have no time to brood over the afterlife."

"I am of an age with each, what matter if my hair turns grey?"

3

清晨,我把漁網撒進大海。我從黑暗的深淵中,拖出一些東西:奇異的形狀,奇異的美麗——有一些照耀著,像微笑;有一些閃爍著,像眼淚;有一些紅暈著,像新娘的臉頰。

我帶著一天的負擔回到家的時候,我的愛人正坐在花園中,悠閒的扯動著片片花葉。

我猶豫片刻,然後把所有打撈起來的東西放在她的腳邊,默默的站在旁邊。她看了那些東西一眼,說:「這些怪東西是什麼?我不知道它們有什麼用!」

我低下頭,羞愧的想:「我不曾為這些東西奮鬥,也沒有到市場上購買它們;它們不是我獻給她的適合的禮物。」

整整一夜,我把它們一件一件的丟到大街上。

清晨,遊客來了,撿起那些東西,把它們帶到遙遠的國度。

THREE

In the morning I cast my net into the sea. I dragged up from the dark abyss things of strange aspect and strange beauty —— some shone like a smile, some glistened like tears, and some were flushed like the cheeks of a bride.

When with the day's burden I went home, my love was sitting in the garden idly tearing the leaves of a flower.

I hesitated for a moment, and then placed at her feet all that I had dragged up, and stood silent. She glanced at them and said, "What strange things are these? I know not of what use they are!"

I bowed my head in shame and thought, "I have not fought for these, I did not buy them in the market; they are not fit gifts for her."

Then the whole night through I flung them one by one into the street.

In the morning travellers came; they picked them up and carried them into far countries.

4

天啊，他們為什麼把我的房子建在通往城鎮的馬路邊？
他們把滿載的船隻停泊在我的樹林附近。
他們隨意的逛來逛去。

我坐下來看著他們，歲月蹉跎了。
我不能回絕他們。於是，我的時間流逝了。
日日夜夜，他們的腳步聲在我的門前響起。
我徒勞的大叫：「我不認識你們。」
有些人是我的手指所認識的，有些人是我的鼻孔所認識
的，我血管中的血液似乎認識他們，有些人是我的睡夢所認識
的。
我不能回絕他們。我叫住他們，說：「誰如果願意的話，
就到我的房子來吧！是的，來吧！」

清晨，寺廟裡的鐘聲響起。
他們手中捧著籃子來了。
他們的腳像玫瑰般紅潤。清晨的微光，灑在他們的臉上。
我不能回絕他們。我叫住他們，說：「到我的花園採集鮮
花吧！到這裡來吧！」

FOUR

Ah me, why did they build my house by the road to the market town?

They moor their laden boats near my trees.

They come and go and wander at their will.

I sit and watch them; my time wears on.

Turn them away I cannot. And thus my days pass by.

Night and day their steps sound by my door.

Vainly I cry, "I do not know you."

Some of them are known to my fingers, some to my nostrils, the blood in my veins seems to know them, and some are known to my dreams.

Turn them away I cannot. I call them and say, "Come to my house whoever chooses. Yes, come."

In the morning the bell rings in the temple.

They came with baskets in their hands.

Their feet are rosy-red. The early light of dawn is on their faces.

Turn them away I cannot. I call them and I say, "Come to my garden to gather flowers! Come hither!"

中午，鑼聲在宮殿門口響起。

我不知道他們為什麼放下手中的工作，在我的籬笆附近徘徊。

他們頭髮上的花朵已經褪色、枯萎了；他們長笛中的音符也顯得疲憊。

我不能回絕他們。我叫住他們，說：「我的樹蔭下是涼爽的。來吧，朋友們。」

夜晚，蟋蟀在樹林中鳴叫。

那是誰啊，緩緩的來到我的門前，輕輕的叩門？

朦朧間，我看到那張臉，他一言不發，四周是一片寂靜的天空。

我不能回絕我的沉靜的客人。透過黑暗，我看著這張臉，夢幻的時光流逝了。

In the mid-day the gong sounds at the palace gate.

I know not why they leave their work and linger near my hedge.

The flowers in their hair are pale and faded; the notes are languid in their flutes.

Turn them away I cannot. I call them and say, "The shade is cool under my trees. Come, friends."

At night the crickets chirp in the woods.

Who is it that comes slowly to my door and gently knocks?

I vaguely see the face, not a word is spoken, the stillness of the sky is all around.

Turn away my silent guest I cannot. I look at the face through the dark, and hours of dreams pass by.

5

　　我的心緒煩亂，渴望著遠方的事物。

　　我的靈魂在渴望中出走，要去觸摸黯淡的遙遠的裙沿。

　　啊，偉大的來生，啊，你笛聲的熱切的呼喚！

　　我忘記了，我總是忘記了，我沒有奮飛的翅膀，我始終被束縛在這個地方。

　　我渴望而清醒，我是一個在陌生土地上的陌生人。

　　你的呼吸向我低語出一個不可能的希望。

　　我的心瞭解你的語言，就像它瞭解自己的語言一樣。

　　啊，遙遠的追尋，啊，你笛聲的熱切的呼喚！

　　我忘記了，我總是忘記了，我不認得路，我沒有生翅的駿馬。

　　我的情緒低落，我是自己心中的流浪者。

　　在疲倦時光的日靄中，你的廣闊幻影在天空的蔚藍中呈現出來！

　　啊，最遙遠的盡頭，啊，你笛聲的熱切的呼喚！

　　我忘記了，我總是忘記了，在我獨居的房子裡，所有的門戶都是緊閉的！

FIVE

I am restless. I am athirst for faraway things.

My soul goes out in a longing to touch the skirt of the dim distance.

O Great Beyond, O the keen call of thy flute!

I forget, I ever forget, that I have no wings to fly, that I am bound in this spot evermore.

I am eager and wakeful, I am a stranger in a strange land.

Thy breath comes to me whispering an impossible hope.

Thy tongue is known to my heart as its very own.

O Far-to-seek, O the keen call of thy flute!

I forget, I ever forget, that I know not the way, that I have not the winged horse.

I am listless, I am a wanderer in my heart.

In the sunny haze of the languid hours, what vast vision of thine takes shape in the blue of the sky!

O Farthest end, O the keen call of thy flute!

I forget, I ever forget, that the gates are shut everywhere in the house where I dwell alone!

6

馴服的鳥兒在籠子裡，自由的鳥兒在森林裡。
時間到了，牠們會相遇，這是命中註定的。

自由的鳥兒大喊：「噢，我的愛人，讓我們飛到樹林裡
吧！」
籠中的鳥兒小聲說：「到這裡來吧，讓我倆都住在籠子裡
吧！」

自由的鳥兒說：「在柵欄中間，哪有展開翅膀的空間
呢？」
「可憐啊，」籠中的鳥兒大喊，「在天空中，我不知道到
哪裡休息。」

SIX

The tame bird was in a cage, the free bird was in the forest.
They met when the time came, it was a decree of fate.

The free bird cries, "O my love, let us fly to wood."
The cage bird whisper, "Come hither, let us both live in the cage."

Says the free bird, "Among bars, where is there room to spread
one's wings?"
"Alas," cries the cage bird, "I should not know where to sit
perched in the sky."

自由的鳥兒大喊：「親愛的，高唱森林之歌吧！」

　　籠中的鳥兒說：「坐在我旁邊吧，我要教你博學者的語言。」

　　森林的鳥兒大喊：「不，絕不！歌曲是不能傳授的。」

　　籠中的鳥兒說：「我的天啊，我不知道什麼是森林之歌。」

　　牠們的愛情在渴望中變得更強烈，但是牠們永遠不能比翼雙飛。

　　牠們隔著籠子看著對方，但是牠們相知的願望只是徒然的。

　　牠們在思慕中拍著翅膀鳴唱：「靠近一些吧，我的愛人！」

　　自由的鳥兒大喊：「不能啊，我害怕這個籠子的緊閉的門。」

　　籠中的鳥兒低聲說：「天啊，我的翅膀沒有力量，已然廢棄。」

The free bird cries, "My darling, sing the songs of the woodlands."

The cage bird says, "Sit by my side, I'll teach you the speech of the learned."

The forest bird cries, "No, ah no! songs can never be taught."

The cage bird says, "Alas for me, I know not the songs of the woodlands."

Their love is intense with longing, but they never can fly wing to wing.

Through the bars of the cage they look, and vain is their wish to know each other.

They flutter their wings in yearning, and sing, "Come closer, my love!"

The free bird cries, "It cannot be, I fear the closed doors of the cage."

The cage bird whispers, "Alas, my wings are powerless and dead."

媽媽啊，年輕的王子要從我們的門前經過——今天早晨我哪有心思工作呢？

教我怎樣編起頭髮；告訴我應該穿哪一件衣裳。

你為什麼驚訝的望著我，媽媽？

我深知他不會瞧我的窗子一眼；我知道他會在轉瞬之間走出我的視線；只有漸弱的笛聲，在遠方朝著我哀泣。

但是，年輕的王子將會從我們的門前經過，我要為那一刻穿上最好的衣裳。

媽媽啊，年輕的王子已經從我們的門前經過了，朝陽在他的戰車上放射出光芒。

我揭開臉上的面紗，扯下我頸上的紅寶石項鏈，拋在他走來的路上。

你為什麼驚訝的望著我，媽媽？

我深知他沒有撿起我的項鏈，我知道它已經被他的車輪輾碎了，留作塵土中的一片紅斑，沒有人知道我的禮物是什麼，或是要給誰。

但是，年輕的王子曾經從我們的門前經過，我曾經把胸前的寶石扔到他面前的路上。

SEVEN

O mother, the young Prince is to pass by our door, —— how can I attend to my work this morning?

Show me how to braid up my hair; tell me what garment to put on.

Why do you look at me amazed, mother?

I know well he will not glance up once at my window; I know he will pass out of my sight in the twinkling of an eye; only the vanishing strain of the flute will come sobbing to me from afar.

But the young Prince will pass by our door, and I will put on my best for the moment.

O mother, the young Prince did pass by our door, and the morning sun flashed from his chariot.

I swept aside the veil from my face, I tore the ruby chain from my neck and flung it in his path.

Why do you look at me amazed, mother?

I know well he did not pick up my chain; I know it was crushed under his wheels leaving a red stain upon the dust, and no one knows what my gift was nor to whom.

But the young Prince did pass by our door, and I flung the jewel from my breast before his path.

8

　　當我床前的燈熄滅的時候，我與晨鳥一起醒來。

　　我坐在打開的窗前，在鬆散的秀髮上戴上鮮嫩的花環。

　　在清晨玫瑰色的薄霧中，年輕的旅人沿路走來。

　　他的頸上掛著一串珍珠，陽光灑在他的花冠上。

　　他在我的門前停下，用急切的呼聲問我：「她在哪裡？」

　　我羞得不能言語：「她是我，年輕的旅人，她就是我啊！」

　　夜幕降臨，燈還沒有點上。

　　我心緒不寧的編著我的髮辮。

　　年輕的旅人駕著戰車，在夕陽的光輝中趕來。

　　他的馬兒口中吐著白沫，他的衣衫上掛著灰塵。

　　他在我的門前跳下車，用疲憊的聲音問：「她在哪裡？」

　　我羞得不能言語：「她是我，疲倦的旅人，她就是我啊！」

　　這是一個四月的夜晚。我的房中點著燈。

　　南方的微風徐徐吹來。聒噪的鸚鵡在牠的籠中睡著了。

　　我的胸衣像孔雀的頸翎一樣的華豔，我的披風像鮮嫩的青草一樣的翠碧。

　　我坐在窗前的地上，凝望著冷清的街道。

　　透過漆黑的夜色，我不停的呢喃：「她是我，絕望的旅人，她就是我啊！」

EIGHT

When the lamp went out by my bed I woke up with the early birds.

I sat at my open window with a fresh wreath on my loose hair.

The young traveller came along the road in the rosy mist of the morning.

A pearl chain was on his neck, and the sun's ray fell on his crown.

He stopped before my door and asked me with an eager cry, "Where is she?"

For very shame I could not say, "She is I, young traveller, she is I."

It was dusk and the lamp was not lit.

I was listlessly braiding my hair.

The young traveller came on his chariot in the glow of the setting sun.

His horses were foaming at the mouth, and there was dust on his gament.

He alighted at my door and asked in a tired voice, "Where is she?"

For very shame I could not say, "She is I, weary traveller, she is I."

It is an April night. The lamp is burning in my room.

The breeze of the south comes gently. The noisy parrot sleeps in its cage.

My bodice is the colour of the peacock's throat, and my mantle is green as young grass.

I sit upon the floor at the window watching the deserted street.

Through the dark night I keep humming, "She is I, despairing traveller, she is I."

9

　　當我在夜晚獨自去約會的時候，鳥兒不鳴，風兒不吹，街道兩旁的房屋靜靜的站著。

　　是我自己的腳鐲越走越響，我羞愧難當。

　　當我坐在陽台上聆聽他的腳步的時候，樹上的葉子紋絲不動，河水靜止得像熟睡的哨兵膝上的刀劍。

　　是我自己的心在瘋狂跳動——我不知道怎樣平息它。

　　當我的愛人過來坐到我身邊的時候，我的身體顫慄著，我的眼瞼低垂著，夜黑了，風吹燈滅，雲片在繁星上曳過面紗。

　　是我自己胸前的珠寶在閃爍與照耀。我不知道怎樣藏起它。

NINE

When I go alone at night to my love-tryst, birds do not sing, the wind does not stir, the houses on both sides of the street stand silent.

It is my own anklets that grow loud at every step and I am ashamed.

When I sit on my balcony and listen for his footsteps, leaves do not rustle on the trees, and the water is still in the river like the sword on the knees of a sentry fallen asleep.

It is my own heart that beats wildly —— I do not know how to quiet it.

When my love comes and sits by my side, when my body trembles and my eyelids droop, the night darkens, the wind blows out the lamp, and the clouds draw veils over the stars.

It is the jewel at my own breast that shines and gives light. I do not know how to hide it.

10

放下你的工作吧，新娘。聽，客人來了。
你聽到了嗎，他在輕輕的搖動閂門的鏈子？

小心你的腳鐲，不要讓它發出太大的聲響；迎接他的時
候，你的腳步不要太急。
放下你的工作吧，新娘，客人在晚上來了。

不，這不是一陣陰風，新娘，不要驚慌。
這是四月夜晚的滿月；庭院中的影子淒清蒼白，頭頂上的
天空明朗清澈。

如果你覺得需要，就用面紗遮住你的臉吧；如果你害怕，
就提著燈到門口吧！

不，這不是一陣陰風，新娘，不要驚慌。

TEN

Let your work be, bride. Listen, the guest has come.

Do you hear, he is gently shaking the chain which fastens the door?

See that your anklets make no loud noise, and that your step is not overhurried at meeting him.

Let your work be, bride, the guest has come in the evening.

No, it is not the ghostly wind, bride, do not be frightened.

It is the full moon on a night of April; shadows are pale in the courtyard; the sky overhead is bright.

Draw your veil over your face if you must, carry the lamp to the door if you fear.

No, it is not the ghostly wind, bride, do not be frightened.

如果你害羞，就不要跟他說話；迎接他的時候，你就站在門邊吧！

如果他問你問題，你可以沉默的低眸，如果你願意。

當你提著燈引他進門的時候，不要讓你的手鐲叮噹作響。

如果你害羞，就不要跟他說話。

你還沒有完成你的工作嗎，新娘？聽，客人來了。

你還沒有把牛棚裡的燈點上嗎？

你還沒有把晚禱的供品籃準備好嗎？

你還沒有把紅色的幸運符繫在你的髮際嗎？你還沒有把你的晚裝整理好嗎？

新娘啊，聽到了嗎，客人來了？

放下你的工作吧！

Have no word with him if you are shy; stand aside by the door when you meet him.

If he asks you questions, and if you wish to, you can lower your eyes in silence.

Do not let your bracelets jingle when, lamp in hand, you lead him in.

Have no word with him if you are shy.

Have you not finished your work yet, bride? Listen, the guest has come.

Have you not lit the lamp in the cowshed?

Have you not got ready the offering basket for the evening service?

Have you not put the red lucky mark at the parting of your hair, and done your toilet for the night?

O bride, do you hear, the guest has come?

Let your work be!

11

　　你就這樣的來吧，不要在梳妝上拖延時間。

　　如果你的髮辮鬆散了，如果你的髮縫歪斜了，如果你的胸衣的絲帶鬆開了，不要在意。

　　你就這樣的來吧，不要在梳妝上拖延時間。

　　來吧，從草地上快步跑來吧！

　　如果你腳上的紅赭石被露水沾掉了，如果你腳踝上的鈴串鬆弛了，如果珍珠從你的鏈子上脫落了，不要在意。

　　來吧，從草地上快步跑來吧！

　　你是否看到烏雲遮住天空？

　　遠遠的河岸上，一群群野鶴飛向天際，一陣陣狂風掃向石南樹叢。

　　受驚的牛羊，衝向村子裡的畜欄。

　　你是否看到烏雲遮住天空？

　　你徒勞的試圖點燃梳妝的燈火——它搖曳著在風中熄滅。

　　誰會知道你的眼瞼上沒有畫眼影？因為你的眼睛比墨雲還黑。

　　你徒勞的試圖點燃梳妝的燈——它熄滅了。

　　你就這樣的來吧，不要在梳妝上拖延時間。

　　如果花環沒有編好，誰會在意呢；如果手鏈沒有繫牢，就由它去吧！

　　天空佈滿烏雲——時間已晚。

　　你就這樣的來吧，不要在梳妝上拖延時間。

ELEVEN

Come as you are; do not loiter over your toilet.

If your braided hair has loosened, if the parting of your hair be not straight, if the ribbons of your bodice be not fastened, do not mind.

Come as you are; do not loiter over your toilet.

Come, with quick steps over the grass.

If the raddle come from your feet because of the dew, if the rings of bells upon your feet slacken, if pearls drop out of your chain, do not mind.

Come with quick steps over the grass.

Do you see the clouds wrapping the sky?

Flocks of cranes fly up from the further river-bank and fitful guests of wind rush over the heath.

The anxious cattle run to their stalls in the village.

Do you see the clouds wrapping the sky?

In vain you light your toilet lamp —— it flickers and goes out in the wind.

Who can know that your eyelids have not been touched with lampblack? For your eyes are darker than rain-clouds.

In vain you light your toilet lamp —— it goes out.

Come as you are; do not loiter over your toilet.

If the wreath is not woven, who cares; if the wrist-chain has not been linked, let it be.

The sky is overcast with clouds —— it is late.

Come as you are; do not loiter over your toilet.

12

　　如果你忙著把你的水瓶灌滿，來吧，到我的湖邊吧！

　　湖水會緊緊擁著你的雙腳，喃喃的傾訴它的秘密。

　　大雨前奏的雲影籠罩著沙灘，烏雲低垂在綠樹勾勒出的青黛的曲線上，彷彿你眉頭上濃密的秀髮。

　　我深知你的腳步的節奏，它們在我的心中敲擊。

　　來吧，到我的湖邊吧，如果你必須把你的水瓶灌滿。

　　如果你想慵懶閒坐，讓你的水瓶在水上漂浮，來吧，到我的湖邊吧！

　　草坡青碧，野花無數。

　　你的思緒將會從你的烏黑眼眸中飛出，就像鳥兒飛出牠們的巢穴。

　　你的面紗將會滑落到你的腳下。

　　來吧，到我的湖邊吧，如果你必須閒坐。

TWELVE

If you would be busy and fill your pitcher, come, O come to my lake.

The water will cling round your feet and babble its secret.

The shadow of the coming rain is on the sands, and the clouds hang low upon the blue lines of the trees like the heavy hair above your eyebrows.

I know well the rhythm of your steps, they are beating in my heart.

Come, O come to my lake, if you must fill your pitcher.

If you would be idle and sit listless and let your pitcher float on the water, come, O come to my lake.

The grassy slope is green, and the wild flowers beyond number.

Your thoughts will stray out of your dark eyes like birds from their nests.

Your veil will drop to your feet.

Come, O come to my lake if you must sit idle.

如果你想拋開遊戲跳進水裡，來吧，到我的湖邊吧！

把你的藍色披風留在岸上，蔚藍的湖水將會把你覆蓋、隱藏。

水波將會躡足來吻你的頸子，在你的耳邊低語。

來吧，到我湖邊來吧，如果你想跳進水裡。

如果你一定要瘋狂而躍向死亡，來吧，到我的湖邊吧！

它清爽冰涼，深邃無底。

它陰沉黑暗，像無夢的睡眠。

在它的深處，黑夜就是白天，歌聲就是靜默。

來吧，到我的湖邊吧，如果你要躍向死亡。

If you would leave off your play and dive in the water, come, O come to my lake.

Let your blue mantle lie on the shore; the blue water will cover you and hide you.

The waves will stand a-tiptoe to kiss your neck and whisper in your ears.

Come, O come to my lake, if you would dive in the water.

If you must be mad and leap to your death, come, O come to my lake.

It is cool and fathomlessly deep.

It is dark like a sleep that is dreamless.

There in its depths nights and days are one, and songs are silence.

Come, O come to my lake, if you would plunge to your death.

13

我別無所求，只站在樹林邊的大樹後面。

黎明的眼睛上還留著倦意，空氣中還帶著露的痕跡。

在地面上的薄霧中，懸掛著潮濕青草的慵懶香氣。

在榕樹下，你正在用雙手擠著牛奶，雙手如凝脂般的柔滑鮮嫩。

我沉靜的站立著。

我一言不發，那是藏在密葉叢中的鳥兒在歌唱。

芒果樹搖落一樹的繁花，灑在鄉間的小路上，一隻隻蜜蜂，嗡嗡的唱著，接踵而至。

在池塘邊，濕婆廟的大門敞開了，朝拜者們已經開始誦經。

你把罐子放在膝上，正在擠著牛奶。

我提著我的空桶站立著。

我沒有靠近你。

天空和寺廟的鑼聲一同響起。

被驅趕的牛群的蹄子，揚起路上的灰塵。

女人們的腰間帶著叮噹作響的水瓶，從河邊走來。

你的手鐲叮叮噹噹，乳沫溢出罐沿。

清晨過去了，我沒有靠近你。

THIRTEEN

I asked nothing, only stood at the edge of the wood behind the tree.

Languor was still upon the eyes of the dawn, and the dew in the air.

The lazy smell of the damp grass hung in the thin mist above the earth.

Under the banyan tree you were milking the cow with your hands, tender and fresh as butter.

And I was standing still.

I did not say a word. It was the bird that sang unseen from the thicket.

The mango tree was shedding its flowers upon the village road, and the bees came humming one by one.

On the side of the pond the gate of Shiva's temple was open and the worshipper had begun his chants.

With the vessel on your lap you were milking the cow.

I stood with my empty can.

I did not come near you.

The sky woke with the sound of the gong at the temple.

The dust was raised in the road from the hoofs of the driven cattle.

With the gurgling pitchers at their hips, women came from the river.

Your bracelets were jingling, and foam brimming over the jar.

The morning wore on and I did not come near you.

14

　　我在路上行走，不知道為什麼，中午過後，竹枝在風中沙沙作響。

　　傾斜的影子伸出臂膀，拖住時光匆匆的腳步。

　　布穀鳥已經厭倦自己的歌聲。

　　我在路上行走，不知道為什麼。

　　水邊的茅屋被懸於頭頂的大樹蔽蔭著。

　　有人正在忙著她的工作，她的腳鐲在角落處響著樂音。

　　我站在這間茅屋前，不知道為什麼。

　　狹窄的小徑蜿蜒著穿過一片片芥菜地，一層層芒果林。

　　它經過村莊的寺廟，經過碼頭的市集。

　　我在這間茅屋前停下，不知道為什麼。

　　多年前，一個微風輕拂的三月天，泉水慵懶的低吟，芒果花飄落在塵土中。

　　細浪騰躍，輕輕拍打著碼頭台階上的銅罐。

　　我回想著微風輕拂的三月天，不知道為什麼。

　　暗影加重，牛羊回欄。

　　孤寂的草地上日色蒼茫，村民們在岸邊等候著渡船。

　　我緩步回去，不知道為什麼。

FOURTEEN

I was walking by the road, I do not know why, when the noonday was past and bamboo branches rustled in the wind.

The prone shadows with their outstretched arms clung to the feet of the hurrying light.

The koels were weary of their songs.

I was walking by the road, I do not know why.

The hut by the side of the water is shaded by an overhanging tree.

Some one was busy with her work, and her bangles made music in the corner.

I stood before this hut, I know not why.

The narrow winding road crosses many a mustard field, and many a mango forest.

It passes by the temple of the village and the market at the river landing place.

I stopped by this but, I do not know why.

Years age it was a day of breezy March when the murmur if the spring was languorous, and mango blossoms were dropping on the dust.

The rippling water leapt and licked the brass vessel that stood on the landing step.

I think of that day of breezy March, I do not know why.

Shadows are deepening and cattle returning to their folds.

The light is grey upon the lonely meadows, and the village are waiting for the ferry at the bank.

I slowly return upon my steps, I do not know why.

15

　　我像麝香鹿一樣在林蔭中奔跑，為自己的香氣而瘋狂。

　　夜晚是五月中旬的夜晚，和風是南方的和風。

　　我迷路了，我遊蕩著，我追尋的是我得不到的東西，我得到的是我不曾追尋的東西。

　　我自己願望的形象，從我的心中走出來跳舞。

　　這個隱約閃爍的幻影，飛掠而出。

　　我試圖緊緊的抓住它，它躲開了，又把我引入歧途。

　　我追尋的是我得不到的東西，我得到的是我不曾追尋的東西。

FIFTEEN

I run as a musk-deer runs in the shadow of the forest mad with his own perfume.

The night is the night of mid-May, the breeze is the breeze of the south.

I lose my way and I wander, I seek what I cannot get, I get what I do not seek.

From my heart comes out and dances the image of my own desire.

The gleaming vision flits on.

I try to clasp it firmly, it eludes me and leads me astray.

I seek what I cannot get, I get what I do not seek.

手牽著手，眼望著眼：就這樣，開始我們的心路歷程。

這是三月一個灑滿月光的夜晚；空氣中飄著散沫花香甜的氣息；我的長笛孤零零的躺在泥土中，你的花串也沒有編好。

你我之間的愛，單純得像一首歌。

你的橘黃色面紗，迷醉我的眼睛。

你編織的茉莉花環像一種榮耀，震顫我的心。

這是一個欲予欲留、忽隱忽現的遊戲；有一些微笑，有一些嬌羞，還有一些甜蜜的無謂的掙扎。

你我之間的愛，單純得像一首歌。

沒有視線之外的神秘；沒有可能之外的強求；沒有魅力背後的陰影；沒有黑暗深處的探索。

你我之間的愛，單純得像一首歌。

我們沒有偏離語言的軌道，陷入永恆的沉默；我們沒有舉起手，向希望之外的空虛奢求。

我們給予的與得到的，已經足夠了。

我們不曾把歡樂徹底輾碎，從中榨出痛苦之酒。

你我之間的愛，單純得像一首歌。

SIXTEEN

Hands cling to hands and eyes linger on eyes: thus begins the record of our hearts.

It is the moonlit night of March; the sweet smell of henna is in the air; my flute lies on the earth neglected and your garland of flowers is unfinished.

This love between you and me is simple as a song.

Your veil of the saffron colour makes my eyes drunk.

The jasmine wreath that you wove me thrills to my heart like praise.

It is a game of giving and withholding, revealing and screening again; some smiles and some little shyness, and some sweet useless struggles.

This love between you and me is simple as a song.

No mystery beyond the present; no striving for the impossible; no shadow behind the charm; no groping in the depth of the dark.

This love between you and me is simple as a song.

We do not stray out of all words into the ever silent; we do not raise our hands to the void for things beyond hope.

It is enough what we give and we get.

We have not crushed the joy to the utmost to wring from it the wine of pain.

This love between you and me is simple as a song.

17

黃鳥在樹上歌唱，讓我的心歡快起舞。
我們兩人住在同一個村莊，這是我們的一份喜悅。
她寵愛的一對小羊，來到我家花園的樹蔭下吃草。
如果牠們闖進我家的麥田，我就把牠們抱在臂彎裡。
我們的村莊叫做康家那，我們的河被稱為安紮那。
我的名字，全村人都知道，而她叫做藍嘉娜。

我們之間，僅隔著一塊田地。
在我家的樹林中築巢的蜜蜂，飛到她們那邊去採蜜。
從她們渡口台階上流來的落花，漂到我們洗澡的小溪中。

SEVENTEEN

The yellow birds sings in their tree and makes my heart dance with gladness.

We both live in the same village, and that is our one piece of joy.

Her pair of pet lambs come to graze in the shade of our garden trees.

If they stray into my barley field, I take them up in my arms.

The name of our village is Khanjana, and Anjana they call our river.

My name is known to all the village, and her name is Ranjana.

Only one field lies between us.

Bees that have hived in our grove go to seek honey in theirs.

Flowers launched from their landing-stairs come floating by the stream where we bathe.

一籃一籃的乾紅花，從他們的田裡送到我們的市集上。
我們的村莊叫做康家那，我們的河被稱為安棻那。
我的名字，全村人都知道，而她叫做藍嘉娜。

伸向她家的那條蜿蜒小路，春天飄滿芒果的花香。
他們的亞麻籽成熟收穫的時候，我們田裡的大麻正在開
花。
在他們的小屋前微笑的星星，也把同樣的閃爍眼神送給我
們。
在他們的池塘裡流溢的雨水，也讓我們的迦懸樹林歡悅。
我們的村莊叫做康家那，我們的河被稱為安棻那。
我的名字，全村人都知道，而她叫做藍嘉娜。

Baskets of dried kusm flowers come from their fields to our market.

The name of our village is Khanjana, and Anjana they call our river.

My name is known to all the village, and her name is Ranjana.

The lane that winds to their house is fragrant in the spring with mango flowers.

When their linseed is ripe for harvest the hemp is in bloom in our field.

The stars that smile on their cottage send us the same twinkling look.

The rain that floods their tank makes glad our kadam forest.

The name of our village is Khanjana, and Anjana they call our river.

My name is known to all the village, and her name is Ranjana.

18

　　當兩姐妹去打水的時候，她們來到這裡，微笑了。

　　她們一定察覺到，每次她們打水的時候，總是有人躲在樹後。

　　兩姐妹互相低語著，當她們來到這裡的時候。

　　她們一定猜到了，每次她們打水的時候，總是有人躲在樹後的秘密。

　　當她們來到這裡的時候，她們的水瓶突然傾倒，水濺了出來。

　　她們一定發現了，每次她們打水的時候，那個總是躲在樹後的人心跳不止。

　　兩姐妹來到這裡的時候，相互交換著眼神，微笑了。

　　她們輕快的腳步裡帶著笑聲，讓這個每次她們打水的時候總是躲在樹後的人神魂顛倒。

EIGHTEEN

When the two sisters go to fetch water, they come to this spot
and they smile.

They must be aware of somebody who stands behind the trees
whenever they go to fetch water.

The two sisters whisper to each other when they pass this spot.

They must have guessed the secret of that somebody who
stands behind the trees whenever they go to fetch water.

Their pitchers lurch suddenly, and water spills when they reach
this spot.

They must have found that somebody's heart is beating who
stands behind the trees whenever they go to fetch water.

The two sisters glance at each other when they come to this spot,
and they smile.

There is a laughter in their swift-stepping feet, which makes con-
fusion in somebody's mind who stands behind the trees whenever
they go to fetch water.

你走在河畔的小路上，腰間帶著滿滿的水瓶。

你為什麼迅速回頭，透過飄動的面紗，窺視我的臉？

這個從幽暗中投來的一瞥，像微風掠過水面，漾起漣漪，捲進昏沉的海岸。

它來到我的身邊，像黃昏的鳥兒，急急的從一扇窗飛到另一扇窗，穿過無燈的房間，消失在黑夜中。

你像山後的一顆星星隱藏著，而我是一個路上的行人。

但是，你為什麼要停一會兒，透過你的面紗，窺視我的臉，當你走在河畔的小路上，腰間帶著滿滿的水瓶的時候。

NINETEEN

You walked by the riverside path with the full pitcher upon your hip.

Why did you swiftly turn your face and peep at me through your fluttering veil?

That gleaming look from the dark came upon me like a breeze that sends a shiver through the sipping water and sweeps away to the shadowy shore.

It came to me like a bird of the evening that hurriedly flies across the lampless room from the one open window to the other, and disappears in the night.

You are hidden like a star behind the hills, and I am a passer-by upon the road.

But why did you stop for a moment and glance at my face through your veil while you walked by the riverside path with the full pitcher upon your hip?

20

一天又一天，他來了又離開。

去吧，我的朋友，把我頭上的一朵花送給他。

如果他問贈花的人是誰，我懇求你不要把我的名字告訴他
——因為他只是來了又離開。

他坐在樹下的塵土裡。

用繁花與密葉在那裡鋪設一個座位，我的朋友。

他的雙眼滿是憂傷，也把憂傷帶到我的心中。

他不說自己的心事；他只是來了又離開。

TWENTY

Day after day he comes and goes away.

Go, and give him a flower from my hair, my friend.

If he asks who was it that sent it, I entreat you do not tell him my name —— for he only comes and goes away.

He sits on the dust under the tree.

Spread there a seat with flowers and leaves, my friend.

His eyes are sad, and they bring sadness to my heart.

He does not speak what he has in mind; he only comes and goes away.

21

　　當天色破曉的時候，這個年輕的流浪者，他為什麼選擇來到我的門前？

　　每次我進出經過他的身邊的時候，我的目光總是被他的面容所吸引。

　　我不知道應該和他說話還是保持沉默。他為什麼選擇來到我的門前？

　　七月的陰夜是黑沉的；秋日的天空是柔和的藍色；南風把春天吹得躁動不安。

　　他每次都用清新的曲調，編織他的歌。

　　我放下工作，滿眼迷茫。他為什麼選擇來到我的門前？

TWENTY-ONE

Why did he choose to come to my door, the wandering youth, when the day dawned?

As I come in and out I pass by him every time, and my eyes are caught by his face.

I know not if I should speak to him or keep silent. Why did he choose to come to my door.

The cloudy nights in July are dark; the sky is soft blue in the autumn; the spring days are restless with the south wind.

He weaves his songs with fresh tunes every time.

I turn from my work and my eyes fill with the mist. Why did he choose to come my door?

當她快步走過我身邊的時候，她的裙緣碰觸到我。

從心中的未知小島上，突然飄來一陣春天的溫馨。

一陣攪擾的紛繁襲我而過，又轉瞬即逝，像一片撕碎的花瓣在風中飄落。

它落在我的心上，像她身體的嘆息，像她心靈的低語。

TWENTY-TWO

When she passed by me with quick steps, the end of her skirt touched me.

From the unknown island of a heart came a sudden warm breath of spring.

A flutter of a flitting touch brushed me and vanished in a moment, like a torn flower petal blown in the breeze.

It fell upon my heart like a sigh of her body and whisper of her heart.

你為什麼悠閒的坐在那裡，把手鐲玩得叮噹作響呢？
灌滿你的水瓶吧，應該回家了。

你為什麼用你的雙手悠閒的撩弄著流水，又不時的窺望著
路上的那個人？
灌滿你的水瓶回家吧！

清晨的時光過去了──沉黑的水繼續奔流著。
波浪悠閒的歡笑著，相互低語著。
流雲聚集在遠方浮起的土地的天邊。
它們悠閒的徘徊著，看著你的臉，微笑著。
灌滿你的水瓶回家吧！

TWENTY-THREE

Why do you sit there and jingle your bracelets in mere idle sport?
Fill your pitcher. It is time for you to come home.

Why do you stir the water with your hands and fitfully glance at
the road for some one in mere idle sport?
Fill your pitcher and come home.

The morning hours pass by —— the dark water flows on.
The waves are laughing and whispering to each other in mere idle
sport.
The wandering clouds have gathered at the edge of the sky on
yonder rise of the land.
They linger and look at your face and smile mere idle sport.
Fill your pitcher and come home.

24

不要把你心中的秘密藏起來，我的朋友！
說給我聽吧，只說給我聽，悄悄的。

你這個笑得這麼溫柔、說得這麼輕軟的人，聽到它的，將
是我的心，而不是我的耳朵。

夜深沉，庭寧靜，鳥巢被睡眠籠罩著。
透過遲疑的淚光，透過沉吟的微笑，透過甜蜜的羞澀與痛
楚，說給我聽吧，說出你心中的秘密。

TWENTY-FOUR

Do not keep to yourself the secret of your heart, my friend!
Say it to me, only to me, in secret.

You who smile so gently, softly whisper, my heart will hear it, not
my ears.

The night is deep, the house is silent, the birds' nests are
shrouded with sleep.
Speak to me through hesitating tears, through faltering smiles,
through sweet shame and pain, the secret of your heart.

25

「到我們這裡來吧，年輕人，說出實情，為什麼你的眼中帶著狂亂？」

「我不知道我喝了什麼野罌粟酒，讓我的眼中帶著狂亂。」

「啊，多難為情！」

「好啦，有些人聰明，有些人愚笨，有些人粗心，有些人謹慎。有些人的眼睛會笑，有些人的眼睛會哭——我的眼中帶著狂亂。」

「年輕人，你為什麼站在樹蔭下，一動也不動？」

「我的腳被我心中的負擔壓得疲憊不堪，所以我站在樹蔭下，一動也不動。」

「啊，多難為情！」

「好啦，有些人一路挺進，有些人流連徘徊，有些人自由放浪，有些人備受羈絆——我的腳被我心中的負擔壓得疲憊不堪。」

TWENTY-FIVE

"Come to us, youth, tell us truly why there is madness in your eyes?"

"I know not what wine of wild poppy I have drunk, that there is this madness in my eyes."

"Ah, shame!"

"Well, some are wise and some foolish, some are watchful and some careless. There are eyes that smile and eyes that weep —— and madness is in my eyes."

"Youth, why do you stand so still under the shadow of the tree?"

"My feet are languid with the burden of my heart, and I stand still in the shadow."

"Ah, shame!"

"Well, some march on their way and some linger, some are free and some are fettered —— and my feet are languid with the burden of my heart."

「從你的慷慨手中所給予的,我都接受。我別無所求。」

「好吧,好吧,我瞭解你,謙卑的乞丐,你乞求的是一個人的全部所有。」

「如果有一朵飄零的花,我會把它戴在心上。」

「但是如果花上有刺呢?」

「我將會忍受。」

「好吧,好吧,我瞭解你,謙卑的乞丐,你乞求的是一個人的全部所有。」

「如果你抬起和善的雙眼,看看我的臉,就算只有一次,也會讓我的生命充滿甜蜜,超越死亡。」

「但是如果那是一個殘忍的眼神呢?」

「我將會讓它永久的刺透我的心。」

「好吧,好吧,我瞭解你,謙卑的乞丐,你乞求的是一個人的全部所有。」

TWENTY-SIX

"What comes from your willing hands I take. I beg for nothing more."

"Yes, yes, I know you, modest mendicant, you ask for all that one has."

"If there be a stray flower for me I will wear it in my heart."

"But if there be thorns?"

"I will endure them."

"Yes, yes, I know you, modest mendicant, you ask for all that one has."

"If but once you should raise your loving eyes to my face it would make my life sweet beyond death."

"But if there be only cruel glances?"

"I will keep them piercing my heart."

"Yes, yes, I know you, modest mendicant, you ask for all that one has."

27

「相信愛情吧，即使它會帶來悲痛。不要關上你的心扉。」

「啊，不，我的朋友，你的語言太晦澀了，我不能理解。」

「我的愛人啊，心兒應該是和一滴眼淚與一首詩歌一起送給人。」

「啊，不，我的朋友，你的語言太晦澀了，我不能理解。」

「歡樂像露珠一樣的脆弱，它在笑聲中就會隕落。悲痛卻是堅強而持久。讓悲傷的愛情在你的眼中甦醒吧！」

「啊，不，我的朋友，你的語言太晦澀了，我不能理解。」

「蓮花在太陽的視野內開放，失去自己的一切所有。在冬日永恆的迷霧中，它將不再含苞。

「啊，不，我的朋友，你的語言太晦澀了，我不能理解。」

TWENTY-SEVEN

"Trust love even if it brings sorrow. Do not close up your heart."

"Ah no, my friend, your words are dark, I cannot understand them."

"The heart is only giving away with a tear and a song, my love."

"Ah no, my friend, your words are dark, I cannot understand them."

"Pleasure is frail like a dewdrop, while it laughs it dies. But sorrow is strong and abiding. Let sorrowful love wake in your eyes."

"Ah no, my friend, your words are dark, I cannot understand them."

"The lotus blooms in the sight of the sun, and loses all that it has. It would not remain in bud in the eternal winter mist."

"Ah no, my friend, your words are dark, I cannot understand them."

　　你的質問的目光是那麼的憂傷。它們探究我的意圖，就像月亮在洞察大海。

　　我已經把我的生命徹底的袒露在你的眼前，沒有隱瞞，沒有保留。這就是你不認識我的原因。

　　如果它只是一塊寶石，我會把它碎成百餘片珠玉，串成項鏈，掛在你的頸上。

　　如果它只是一朵鮮花，圓潤、嬌小、甜美，我會把它從枝頭上採下，插在你的秀髮上。

　　但是，我的愛人啊，它是一顆心。哪裡是它的海岸，哪裡是它的盡頭？

　　你不知道這個王國的疆界，但是你仍然是它的女王。

　　如果它只是片刻的歡樂，它會在從容的微笑中開花，你就會立刻看到它，讀懂它。

　　如果它只是一陣痛楚，它會融化成清澈的淚水，無言的反射出心底最深處的秘密。

　　但是，我的愛人啊，它是愛。

　　它的歡樂和痛苦是無邊無際的，它的渴求與財富是無窮無盡的。

　　它與你親近得像你的生命一樣，但是你永遠不能完全瞭解它。

TWENTY-EIGHT

Your questioning eyes are sad. They seem to know my meaning as the moon would fathom the sea.

I have bared my life before your eyes from end to end, with nothing hidden or held back. That is why you know me not.

If it were only a gem I could break it into a hundred pieces and string them into a chain to put on your neck.

If it were only a flower, round and small and sweet, I could pluck it from its stem to set it in your hair.

But it is a heart, my beloved. Where are its shores and its bottom?

You know not the limits of this kingdom, still you are its queen.

If it were only a moment of pleasure it would flower in an easy smile, and you could see it and read it in a moment.

If it were merely a pain it would melt in limpid tears, reflecting its inmost secret without a word.

But it is love, my beloved.

Its pleasure and pain are boundless, and endless its wants and wealth.

It is as near to you as your life, but you can never wholly know it.

　　對我說吧，我的愛人！用話語告訴我，你唱的是什麼。
　　夜色漆黑。星星迷失在雲裡。風在樹葉間嘆息。

　　我將會鬆開我的秀髮。我的藍色披風將會像黑夜一樣，緊緊的纏繞我。我將會把你的頭貼在我的胸前：在甜蜜的孤寂中，在你的心頭低訴。我將會閉目聆聽。我不會端詳你的臉。

　　當你的話語結束的時候，我們將會沉默凝坐。只有樹木在黑暗中低吟。
　　夜色將會變得蒼白。天將破曉。我們將會看著彼此的眼睛，然後踏上不同的旅程。

　　對我說吧，我的愛人！用話語告訴我，你唱的是什麼。

TWENTY-NINE

Speak to me, my love! Tell me in words what you sang.

The night is dark. The stars are lost in clouds. The wind is sighing through the leaves.

I will let loose my hair. My blue cloak will cling round me like night. I will clasp your head to my bosom; and there in the sweet loneliness murmur on your heart. I will shut my eyes and listen. I will not look in your face.

When your words are ended, we will sit still and silent. Only the trees will whisper in the dark.

The night will pale. The day will dawn. We shall look at each other's eyes and go on our different paths.

Speak to me, my love! Tell me in words what you sang.

你是夜晚的雲，飄拂在我夢想中的天空。

我永遠用我的愛情的渴望來描繪你、塑造你。

你是我一個人的，僅僅是我一個人的，我無邊無際的夢幻中的居住者！

你的雙腳被我的心的渴望之光染得緋紅，我的夕陽之歌的採集者！

你的雙唇在我的痛苦之酒中，苦澀而甜蜜。

你是我一個人的，僅僅是我一個人的，我孤獨寂寞的夢幻中的居住者！

我用激情的陰影染黑你的眼睛，出沒於我凝望深處的人！

我的愛人，在我的音樂之網中，我抓住你，裹住你。

你是我一個人的，僅僅是我一個人的，我不死不滅的夢幻中的居住者！

THIRTY

You are the evening cloud floating in the sky of my dreams.
I paint you and fashion you ever with my love longings.
You are my own, my own, Dweller in my endless dreams!

Your feet are rosy-red with the glow of my heart's desire, Gleaner
of my sunset songs!
Your lips are bitter-sweet with the taste of my wine of pain.
You are my own, my own, Dweller in my lonesome dreams!

With the shadow of my passion have I darken your eyes,
Haunter of the depth of my gaze!
I have caught you and wrapt you, my love, in the net of my music.
You are my own, my own, Dweller in my deathless dreams!

31

我的心，這隻荒野之鳥，在你的雙眼中，發現了藍天。
它們是清晨的搖籃，它們是群星的王國。
我的詩歌迷失在它們的深淵中。

就讓我在天空中飛翔，在它的孤寂浩瀚中。
就讓我穿破它的雲層，在它的陽光中展開翅膀。

THIRTY-ONE

My heart, the bird of the wilderness, has found its sky in your eyes.

They are the cradle of the morning, they are the kingdom of the stars.

My songs are lost in their depths.

Let me but soar in that sky, in its lonely immensity.

Let me but cleave its clouds and spread wings in its sunshine.

32

告訴我，這一切是否都是真的，我的愛人，告訴我，這是否是真的。

當這一對眼睛閃出電光的時候，在你胸中的烏雲就會做出風暴般的回答。

我的雙唇是否真的像剛剛綻放的初戀的花蕾一樣甜美？

消失的五月的記憶，是否仍然流連於我的肢體？

大地是否像豎琴一樣，在我的雙腳撫弄下，震顫成歌曲？

當我到來的時候，露珠從夜的眼睛中滴落，晨光真的會因為圍繞我的身體而歡躍異常嗎？

是真的嗎，是真的嗎，你的愛是否獨自穿越生生世世來追覓我？

當你最終找到我的時候，你的歲月般久遠的渴望，在我的輕柔低語中，在我的柔滑秀髮中，在我的雙眸裡，在我的朱唇間，是否找到完全的平和？

那個無限的神秘，是否真的寫在我的小小的額頭上？

告訴我，我的愛人，這些是否都是真的。

THIRTY-TWO

Tell me if this be all true, my lover, tell me if this be true.

When these eyes flash their lightning the dark clouds in your breast make stormy answer.

Is it true that my lips are sweet like the opening bud of the first conscious love?

Do the memories of vanished months of May linger in my limbs?

Does the earth, like a sharp, shiver into songs with the touch of my feet?

Is it then true that the dewdrops fall from the eyes of night when I am seen, and the morning light is glad when it wraps my body round?

Is it true, is it true, that your love travelled alone through ages and worlds in search of me?

That when you found me at last, your age-long desire found utter peace in my gentle speech and my eyes and lips and flowing hair?

Is it then true that the mystery of the Infinite is written on this little forehead of mine?

Tell me, my lover, if all this be true.

我愛你，心愛的人。請寬恕我的愛。

像一隻迷路的鳥兒，我被捕獲了。

當我的心在顫抖的時候，它丟掉面紗，赤裸裸的呈現出來。用憐憫遮住它吧，心愛的人，請寬恕我的愛。

如果你不能愛我，心愛的人，請寬恕我的痛苦。

不要從遠處斜眼看我。

我將會偷偷的回到我的角落，在黑暗中獨坐。

我將會用雙手遮住我的赤裸的羞慚。

轉過你的臉，心愛的人，請寬恕我的痛苦。

如果你愛我，心愛的人，請寬恕我的快樂。

當我的心被幸福的洪水捲走的時候，不要笑我危險的放縱。

當我坐上我的寶座，用我專制的愛來統治你的時候，當我像女神一樣，把我的寵愛恩賜於你的時候，請忍受我的驕傲，心愛的人，請寬恕我的快樂。

THIRTY-THREE

I love you, beloved. Forgive me my love.
Like a bird losing its way I am caught.
When my heart was shaken it lost its veil and was naked. Cover it
with pity, beloved, and forgive me my love.

If you cannot love me, beloved, forgive me my pain.
Do not look askance at me from afar.
I will steal back to my corner and sit in the dark.
With both hands I will cover my naked shame.
Turn your face from me, beloved, and forgive me my pain.

If you love me, loved, forgive me my joy.
When my heart is borne away by the flood of happiness, do not
smile at my perilous abandonment.
When I sit on my throne and rule you with my tyranny of love,
when like a goddess I grant you my favor, bear with my pride, beloved,
and forgive me my joy.

不要走，我的愛人，不要不辭而別。

我已經守候了整整一夜，此刻我的眼睛被困倦壓得沉重。

我害怕我睡著的時候，我會失去你。

不要走，我的愛人，不要不辭而別。

我驚跳起來，伸手觸摸你。我問自己：「這是一個夢嗎？」

但願我可以用我的心纏住你的雙足，把它們緊緊的抱在我的胸前！

不要走，我的愛人，不要不辭而別。

THIRTY-FOUR

Do not go, my love, without asking my leave.
I have watched all night, and now my eyes are heavy with sleep.
I fear lest I lose you when I am sleeping.

Do not go, my love, without asking my leave.
I start up and stretch my hands to touch you. I ask myself, "Is it a dream?"
Could I but entangle your feet with my heart and hold them fast to my breast!

Do not go, my love, without asking my leave.

35

唯恐我太容易的認識你，你會對我耍花樣。
你用歡笑的閃光，迷眩我的雙眼，遮掩你的淚水。
我知道，我知道你的把戲。
你的話語，從來就不是你的心中所想。

唯恐我不珍視你，你就千方百計的閃避我。
唯恐我把你與眾人混淆，你獨自站在一旁。
我知道，我知道你的把戲。
你走的路，從來就不是你的心中所願。

你的要求多於別人，所以你才會保持沉默。
你用嬉笑的漫不經心，迴避我的贈與。
我知道，我知道你的把戲。
你接受的，從來就不是你的心中所求。

THIRTY-FIVE

Lest I should know you too easily, you play with me.
You blind me with flashes of laughter to hide your tears.
I know, I know your art.
You never say the word you would.

Lest I should not prize you, you elude me in a thousand ways.
Lest I should confuse you with the crowd, you stand aside.
I know, I know your art.
You never walk the path you would.

Your claim is more than that of others, that is why you are silent.
With playful carelessness you avoid my gifts.
I know, I know your art.
You never will take what you would.

他低語：「我的愛人，抬起眼睛吧！」

我厲聲斥責他，說：「走！」他卻一動也不動。

他站在我的面前，拉起我的雙手。我說：「走開！」他卻沒有走。

他把他的臉靠近我的耳朵。我瞥了他一眼，說：「不要臉！」他卻沒有動。

他的嘴唇碰觸到我的臉頰。我顫抖著說：「你太過份了。」他卻毫不羞慚。

他把一朵花戴到我的頭上。我說：「沒有用的！」他卻站著不動。

他取下我的頸上的花環離去了。我流著眼淚，問自己的心：「他為什麼不回來？」

THIRTY-SIX

He whispered, "My love, raise your eyes."
I sharply chid him, and said "Go!"; but he did not stir.

He stood before me and held both my hands. I said, "Leave me!";
but he did not go.

He brought his face near my ear. I glanced at him and said, "What
a shame!"; but he did not move.

His lips touched my cheek. I trembled and said, "You dare too
much!"; but he had no shame.

He put a flower in my hair. I said, "It is useless!"; but he stood
unmoved.

He took the garland from my neck and went away. I weep and ask
my heart, "Why does he not come back?"

你願意把你的鮮花的花環戴在我的頸上嗎，美麗的人兒？

但是，你必須明白，我的這個花環是為很多人編的，是為那些偶然瞥見的人編的，是為那些居於蠻荒之地的人編的，是為那些住在詩人歌曲中的人編的。

現在要求我的心作為回贈，已經太遲了。

曾經，我的生命像一朵待放的花蕾，所有的芬芳都藏在它的花心中。

現在，它們已經四散遠揚。

誰知道有什麼魅力，可以將它們重新聚集封存？

我的心不能容我只給一個人，它是要給很多人的。

THIRTY-SEVEN

Would you put your wreath of fresh flowers on my neck, fair one?

But you must know that the one wreath that I had woven is for the many, for those who are seen in glimpses, or dwell in lands unexplored, or live in poets' songs.

It is too late to ask my heart in return for yours.

There was a time when my life was like a bud, all its perfume was stored in its core.

Now it is squandered far and wide.

Who knows the enchantment that can gather and shut it up again?

My heart is not mine to give to one only, it is given to the many.

38

　　我的愛人，曾經，你的詩人把一首壯麗的史詩，投進他的心中。

　　天啊，我不小心，它打到你的叮叮噹噹的腳鐲上，引發了哀愁。

　　它破裂成詩歌的碎片，散落在你的腳下。

　　我的那輛滿載古老戰爭傳說的大車，全部被笑聲的浪濤所傾覆，在淚水的浸泡中而沉沒。

　　你一定要好好的補償我的損失，我的愛人。

　　如果，我對死後的不朽名望的追求破滅了，那就讓我在活著的時候永恆吧！

　　我將不會為我的損失而哀痛，也不會責怪你。

THIRTY-EIGHT

My love, once upon a time your poet launched a great epic in his mind.

Alas, I was not careful, and it struck your ringing anklets and came to grief.

It broke up into scraps of songs and lay scattered at your feet.

All my cargo of the stories of old wars was tossed by the laughing waves and soaked in tears and sank.

You must make this loss good to me, my love.

If my claims to immortal fame after death are shattered, make me immortal while I live.

And I will not mourn for my loss nor blame you.

　　整個早晨，我都在試著編一個花環，但是花兒總是滑落出來。

　　你坐在那裡，透過窺探的眼角，偷偷的看著我。

　　問問這一對黑亮頑皮的眼睛，這是誰的錯。

　　我想唱一首歌，卻唱不出來。

　　一抹偷偷的微笑，在你的雙唇上顫抖，問問它我失敗的原因吧！

　　讓你的微笑雙唇發一個誓，證明我的歌聲怎樣迷失在沉默裡，像一隻沉醉在蓮花裡的蜜蜂。

　　天黑了，花兒應該收攏起她們的花瓣。

　　請容許我坐在你的旁邊，吩咐我的雙唇去做在沉靜中與在幽暗的星光中可以做的工作吧！

THIRTY-NINE

I try to weave a wreath all the morning, but the flowers slip and they drop out.

You sit there watching me in secret through the corner of your prying eyes.

Ask those eyes, darkly planning mischief, whose fault it was.

I try to sing a song, but in vain.

A hidden smile trembles on your lips, ask of it the reason of my failure.

Let your smiling lips say on oath how my voice lost itself in silence like a drunken bee in the lotus.

It is evening, and the time for the flowers to close their petals.

Give me leave to sit by your side, and bid my lips to do the work that can be done in silence and in dim light of stars.

40

當我來與你告別的時候，一個疑惑的微笑在你的眼中閃過。

我這樣做的次數太多了，你會認為我很快又會回來。

說實話吧，我的心中也有同樣的懷疑。

因為，春天去了，總會再來；月兒缺了，總會再圓；花兒謝了，還會在枝頭上重綻紅顏，一年又一年。我與你道別，很可能只是為了再回到你的身邊。

但是，把這個幻影保留一刻吧；不要粗魯、匆忙的把它趕走。

當我說我要永遠離開你的時候，你就把它當作是真的吧，讓淚水的迷霧暫時加深你的眼邊的黑影。

當我再次回來的時候，隨便你怎樣的狡猾微笑吧！

FORTY

An unbelieving smile flits on your eyes when I come to you to take my leave.

I have done it so often that you think I will soon return.

To tell you the truth I have the same doubt in my mind.

For the spring days come again time after time; the full moon takes leave and comes on another visit, the flower come again and blush upon their branches year after year, and it is likely that I take my leave only to come to you again.

But keep the illusion awhile; do not send it away with ungentle haste.

When I say I leave you for all time, accept it as true, and let a mist of tears for one moment deepen the dark rim of your eyes.

Then smile as archly as you like when I come again.

　　我渴望著對你說出我要說的最深處的話語；但是我不敢，我害怕你嘲笑。

　　因此，我嘲笑自己，把我的秘密在戲謔中摔碎。

　　我輕描淡寫自己的痛苦，因為我害怕你會這樣做。

　　我渴望著告訴你我要說的最真實的話語；但是我不敢，我害怕你不相信。

　　因此，我用謊言偽裝它們，說出和內心相反的話。

　　我讓自己的痛苦顯得可笑，因為我害怕你會這樣做。

　　我渴望著用最珍貴的詞語來形容你；但是我不敢，我害怕無法得到相應的回報。

　　因此，我給你刻薄的綽號，以誇耀我的冷酷力量。

　　我傷害你，因為我害怕你永遠不知道痛苦。

　　我渴望著默默的坐在你的身邊；但是我不敢，我害怕我的心兒會跳到我的唇上。

　　因此，我輕鬆的東拉西扯，把我的心藏在話語的後面。

　　我粗暴的對待我的痛苦，因為我害怕你會這樣做。

　　我渴望著從你的身邊走開；但是我不敢，我害怕我的怯懦會被你發現。

　　因此，我高高的昂起頭，毫不在乎的走到你的面前。

　　從你的眼中頻頻射來的錐刺，讓我的痛苦永遠鮮潤。

FORTY-ONE

I long to speak the deepest words I have to say to you; but I dare not, for fear you should laugh.

That is why I laugh at myself and shatter my secret in jest.

I make light of my pain, afraid you should do so.

I long to tell you the truest words I have to say you; but I dare not, being afraid that you would not believe them.

That is why I disguise them in untruth, saying the contrary of what I mean.

I make my pain appear absurd, afraid that you should do so.

I long to use the most precious words I have for you; but I dare not, fearing I should not be paid with like value.

That is why I gave you hard names and boast of my callous strength.

I hurt you, for fear you would never know any pain.

I long to sit silent by you; but I dare not lest my heart come out at my lips.

That is why I prattle and chatter lightly and hide my heart behind words.

I rudely handle my pain, for fear you should do so.

I long to go away from your side; but I dare not, for fear my cowardice should become known to you.

That is why I hold my head high and carelessly come into your presence.

Constant thrusts from your eyes keep my pain fresh for ever.

哦，瘋狂的、雄壯的醉漢；

如果你踢開自己的大門，在眾人的面前裝瘋賣傻；

如果你在夜間傾空包裹，對謹慎不屑的彈起響指；

如果你走上荒誕的道路，與無益的東西糾纏嬉戲；不理會韻律與理性；

如果你在風暴前扯起風帆，把船舵拆成兩半，

那麼，我就會跟隨你，夥伴，一起酩酊大醉，一起跌入墮落。

我曾經在穩重聰明的鄰居間虛度年華。

冗雜的知識，染白我的頭髮；紛繁的觀察，令我兩眼昏花。

多年以來，我積攢了許多零星瑣碎的東西。

把它們輾碎，在上面跳舞，讓它們隨風飄散。

因為我知道，酩酊大醉並且跌入墮落，才是最高的智慧。

FORTY-TWO

O mad, superbly drunk;
If you kick open your doors and play the fool in public;
If you empty your bag in a night, and snap your fingers at
prudence;
If you walk in curious paths and play with useless things;
Reck not rhyme or reason;
If unfurling your sails before the storm you snap the rudder in
two,
Then I will follow you, comrade, and be drunken and go to the
dogs.

I have wasted my days and nights in the company of steady wise
neighbors.
Much knowing has turned my hair grey, and much watching has
made my sight dim.

For years I have gathered and heaped up scraps and fragments
of things;
Crush them and dance upon them, and scatter them all to the
winds.
For I know 'tis the height of wisdom to be drunken and go to the
dogs.

讓一切扭曲的顧慮消亡吧，讓我絕望的迷路吧！

讓一陣旋風捲來，將我與我的鐵錨一起掃走。

知名的人、勞動的人、有用的人、聰明的人，充斥著這個世界。

有些人從容的領頭帶隊，有些人體面的尾隨其後。

讓他們幸福成功，讓我們呆傻無用。

因為我知道，酩酊大醉並且跌入墮落，才是所有工作的終結。

我發誓，此刻，我把所有的欲求都讓給謙謙君子。

我放棄我的學識的驕傲與是非的判斷。

我將會打碎記憶的陶罐，揮灑最後一滴眼淚。

我將會在紅果酒的泡沫中沐浴，並且用它照亮我的歡笑。

我將會把文明與沉靜的徽章撕成碎片。

我將會發誓做一個無用之人，酩酊大醉，跌入墮落。

Let all crooked scruples vanish, let me hopelessly lose my way.

Let a gust of wild giddiness come and sweep me away from my anchors.

The world is peopled with worthies, and workers, useful and clever.

There are men who are easily first, and men who come decently after.

Let them be happy and prosper, and let me be foolishly futile.

For I know 'tis the end of all works to be drunken and go to the dogs.

I swear to surrender this moment all claims to the ranks of the decent.

I let go my pride of learning and judgment of right and of wrong.

I'll shatter memory's vessel, scattering the last the drop of tears.

With the foam of the berry-red wine I will bathe and brighten my laughter.

The badge of the civil and staid I'll tear into shreds for the nonce.

I'll take the holy vow to be worthless, to be drunken and go to the dogs.

43

　　不，我的朋友，我永遠不會做一個苦行僧，隨便你怎麼說吧！

　　我永遠不會做一個苦行僧，如果她不和我一同受戒。

　　這是我的堅定決心，如果我找不到一處陰涼的住處和一個懺悔的伴侶，我永遠不會做一個苦行僧。

　　不，我的朋友，我永遠不會離開我的爐灶與家庭，去密林隱退；如果在林蔭中沒有歡笑的迴盪；如果沒有鬱金香的披風在風中飄揚；如果它的寂靜不會因為輕柔的耳語而倍顯寂靜。

　　我永遠不會做一個苦行僧。

FORTY-THREE

No, my friends, I shall never be an ascetic, whatever you may say.

I shall never be an ascetic if she does not take the vow with me.

It is my firm resolve that if I cannot find a shady shelter and a companion for my penance, I shall never turn ascetic.

No, my friends, I shall never leave my hearth and home, and retire into the forest solitude, if rings no merry laughter in its echoing shade and if the end of no saffron mantle flutters in the wind; if its silence is not deepened by soft whispers.

I shall never be an ascetic.

44

　　尊敬的長者，請寬恕這一對罪人吧！今天，春風狂野的旋舞，捲走塵土和枯葉，你的教誨也隨之消散。

　　神父啊，不要說生命是一場虛空。
　　因為我們曾經一度與死亡休戰，在那個短暫的芬芳的日子裡，我們兩人曾經得到永生。

　　即使是國王的軍隊兇猛的前來追捕，我們會悲哀的搖著頭說，兄弟們，你們打擾了我們。如果你們一定要玩這個聒噪的遊戲，就到別的地方去敲擊你們的武器吧！因為我們剛在這轉瞬即逝的時光中，得到永生。

　　如果友善的人們過來把我們圍攏，我們會謙恭的對他們鞠躬施禮說，這個莫大的榮幸，令我們慚愧。在我們居住的無限天空中，沒有多大的空間。因為春天繁花盛開，蜜蜂的忙碌翅膀也彼此推擠。我們那個小小的天堂，只住著我們兩個永生的人，真的是狹小得可笑。

FORTY-FOUR

Reverend sir, forgive this pair of sinners. Spring winds today are blowing in wild eddies, driving dust and dead leaves away, and with them your lessons are all lost.

Do not say, father, that life is a vanity.

For we have made truce with death for once, and only for a few fragrant hours we two have been made immortal.

Even if the king's army came and fiercely fell upon us we should sadly shake our heads and say, Brothers, you are disturbing us. If you must have this noisy game, go and clatter your arms elsewhere. Since only for a few fleeting moments we have been made immortal.

If friendly people came and flocked around us, we should humbly bow to them and say, This extravagant good fortune is an embarrassment to us. Room is scarce in the infinite sky where we dwell. For in the springtime flowers come in crowds, and the busy wings of bees jostle each other. Our little heaven, where dwell only we two immortals, is too absurdly narrow.

45

　　對那些一定要離開的賓客們，懇求上帝讓他們趕快走，並且掃掉他們的一切足跡。

　　把那些從容的、單純的、親近的微笑，擁入你的懷中。

　　今天是不知道自己死期的幻影的節日。

　　讓你的笑聲只作為無意義的歡樂，像粼粼的波光。

　　讓你的生命像葉尖上的露珠一樣，在時光的邊緣上輕輕起舞。

　　在你的琴弦上，彈出斷續不定的節奏吧！

FORTY-FIVE

To the guests that must go bid God's speed and brush away all traces of their steps.

Take to your bosom with a smile what is easy and simple and near.

Today is the festival of phantoms that know not when they die.

Let your laughter be but a meaningless mirth like twinkles of light on the ripples.

Let your life lightly dance on the edges of Time like dew on the tip of a leaf.

Strike in chords from your harp fitful momentary rhythms.

你離我而去,踏上自己的路途。

我想我將會為你悲傷,還會在我的心中用金色的詩歌鑄成你的孤獨形象。

但是,唉,我的運氣多麼差,時間多麼短暫。

青春一年一年的消逝;春日飄忽短暫;脆弱的花朵無意義的凋謝,聰明的人警告我,生命只是一顆荷葉上的露珠。

我應不應該忽視這一切,凝望那個人離我而去的背影?

那將會是粗魯的、愚蠢的,因為時間多麼短暫。

那麼,來吧,我那伴著急促腳步的雨夜;笑吧,我的金色的秋天;來吧,無憂無慮的四月,到處拋擲你的親吻吧!

你來吧,還有你,也有你!

我的心愛的人們,你們知道我們都是凡人。為了一個帶走她的心的人而心碎,明智嗎?因為時間多麼短暫。

坐在角落裡沉思,用韻律寫出佔有我的全部世界的你們,有多麼甜美啊!

緊抱著自己的悲痛,決定不去接受撫慰,是多麼勇敢啊!

但是,有一張清新的面龐在我的門上窺望,抬起眼看向我的眼睛。

我只能拭去淚水,改變我的歌聲的曲調。

因為時間多麼短暫。

FORTY-SIX

You left me and went on your way.

I thought I should mourn for you and set your solitary image in my heart wrought in a golden song.

But ah, my evil fortune, time is short.

Youth wanes year after year; the spring days are fugitive; the frail flowers die for nothing, and the wise man warns me that life is but a dew-drop on the lotus leaf.

Should I neglect all this to gaze after one who has turned her back on me?

That would be rude and foolish, for time is short.

Then, come, my rainy nights with pattering feet; smile, my golden autumn; come, careless April, scattering your kisses abroad.

You come, and you, and you also!

My loves, you know we are mortals. Is it wise to break one's heart for the one who takes her heart away? For time is short.

It is sweet to sit in a corner to muse and write in rhymes that you are all my world.

It is heroic to hug one's sorrow and determine not to be consoled.

But a fresh face peeps across my door and raises its eyes to my eyes.

I cannot but wipe away my tears and change the tune of my song.

For time is short.

如果你願意這樣，我就會停止歌唱。

如果它讓你的心兒激盪，我就會把目光從你的臉上移開。

如果它在你走路的時候會驚嚇到你，我就會移開腳步走其他的路。

如果它在你編花環的時候會讓你慌亂，我就會避開你的偏僻的花園。

如果它會讓水花肆意飛濺，我就不會沿著你的堤岸划船。

FORTY-SEVEN

If you would have it so, I will end my singing.

If it sets your heart aflutter, I will take away my eyes from your face.

If it suddenly startles you in your walk, I will step aside and take another path.

If it confuses you in your flower-weaving, I will shun your lonely garden.

If it makes the water wanton and wild, I will not row my boat by your bank.

　　把我從你的甜蜜束縛中釋放出來吧，我的愛人！不要再斟上親吻的酒。

　　濃香的煙霧，窒息我的心。
打開門，讓晨光進入吧！

　　我迷失在你當中，被你的重重疊疊的愛撫包圍。
　　把我從你的魔咒中釋放出來吧，把男子氣概交還我，好讓我把自由的心奉獻給你。

FORTY-EIGHT

Free me from the bonds of your sweetness, my love! No more of this wine of kisses.

This mist of heavy incense stifles my heart.
Open the doors, make room for the morning light.

I am lost in you, wrapped in the folds of your caresses.
Free me from your spells, and give me back the manhood to offer you my freed heart.

49

我握住她的手,把她緊緊的抱在胸前。

我試圖用她的魅力填滿我的懷抱,用親吻劫奪她的甜蜜微
笑,用我的眼睛啜飲她的深黑瞥視。

啊,但是,它在哪裡?誰可以從天空淬出蔚藍?

我試圖抓住美麗,它躲開我,只留下軀殼在我的手裡。

我因為失落而困乏的回來。

軀殼怎麼可能觸到只有靈魂才可以觸到的花朵?

FORTY-NINE

I hold her hands and press her to my breast.

I try to fill my arms with her loveliness, to plunder her sweet smile with kisses, to drink her dark glances with my eyes.

Ah, but, where is it? Who can strain the blue from the sky?

I try to grasp the beauty, it eludes me, leaving only the body in my hands.

Baffled and weary I come back.

How can the body touch the flower which only the spirit may touch?

50

愛，我的心日夜都渴望著與你相見——那像吞沒一切的死亡般的相見。

像一陣風暴把我捲走；把我的一切都帶走；劈開我的睡眠，搶走我的夢。把我的世界從我的身邊劫走。

在那個毀滅中，在靈魂的赤裸中，讓我們在美麗中，合而為一。

天啊，我徒然的渴望！除了在你這裡，哪裡還有可以融為一體的希望，我的上帝？

FIFTY

Love, my heart longs day and night for the meeting with you——
for the meeting that is like all-devouring death.

Sweep me away like a storm; take everything I have; break open
my sleep and plunder my dreams. Rob me of my world.

In that devastation, in the utter nakedness of spirit, let us become one in beauty.

Alas for my vain desire! Where is this hope for union except in
thee, my God?

那麼，唱完最後一首歌，就讓我們離開吧！
當夜已不再的時候，就忘記這個夜晚吧！

我曾經試圖把誰擁在臂彎？夢永遠不可能被俘獲。
我的渴求的雙手把虛空壓在心上，它卻壓碎我的胸口。

FIFTY-ONE

Then finish the last song and let us leave.
Forget this night when the night is no more.

Whom do I try to clasp in my arms? Dreams can never be made captive.

My eager hands press emptiness to my heart and it bruises my breast.

燈為什麼熄了？
我用披風遮住它，給它擋風，因此燈就熄了。

花兒為什麼謝了？
我懷著焦灼的愛，把它貼在心上，因此花兒就謝了。

河流為什麼乾了？
我用堤壩把它攔起來，想為我所用，因此河流就乾了。

琴弦為什麼斷了？
我強撥一個超出它的能力範圍的音符，因此琴弦就斷了。

FIFTY-TWO

Why did the lamp go out?

I shaded it with my cloak to save it from the wind, that is why the lamp went out.

Why did the flower fade?

I pressed it to my heart with anxious love, that is why the flower faded.

Why did the stream dry up?

I put a dam across it to have it for my use, that is why the stream dried up.

Why did the harp-string break?

I tried to force a note that was beyond its power, that is why the harp-string is broken.

你為什麼要盯著我,讓我羞怯呢?

我不是來乞討的。

我站在你的庭院外面的花園的籬笆前,只是為了打發時間。

你為什麼要盯著我,讓我羞怯呢?

我沒有從你的花園中採走一朵玫瑰,沒有摘下一顆果實。

在路邊那個每個陌生的旅人都可以站立的陰涼下,我只是謙卑的找一個庇護。

我沒有採走一朵玫瑰。

是的,我的腳累了,大雨也瓢潑而下。

風在搖晃的竹林中呼嘯。

雲像敗軍潰逃似的掠過天空。

我的腳累了。

我不知道你是如何看待我,或是你在門口等著誰。

閃電迷眩你的守望的眼睛。

我如何知道,你是否可以看見站在黑暗中的我?

我不知道你是如何看待我。

一天結束了,雨暫時停了。

我離開你的花園盡頭的樹蔭和草地上的座位。

天色已暗;關上你的門吧;我走我的路。

一天結束了。

FIFTY-THREE

Why do you put me to shame with a look?

I have not come as a beggar.

Only for a passing hour I stood at the end of your courtyard outside the garden hedge.

Why do you put me to shame with a look?

Not a rose did I gather from your garden, not a fruit did I pluck.

I humbly took my shelter under the wayside shade where every strange traveller may stand.

Not a rose did I pluck.

Yes, my feet were tired, and the shower of rain came down.

The winds cried out among the swaying bamboo branches.

The clouds ran across the sky as though in the flight from defeat.

My feet were tired.

I know not what you thought of me or for whom you were waiting at your door.

Flashes of lightning dazzled your watching eyes.

How could I know that you could see me where I stood in the dark?

I know not what you thought of me.

The day is ended, and the rain has ceased for a moment.

I leave the shadow of the tree at the end of your garden and this seat on the grass.

It has darkened; shut your door; I go my way.

The day is ended.

市集已過，你在夜晚提著籃子匆忙的要到哪裡呢？
他們都挑著擔子回家了；月亮在村子樹林的上空窺望著。

呼喚渡船的回音，掠過灰暗的水面，飄向遠方野鴨酣眠的
沼澤。
市集已過，你提著籃子匆忙的要到哪裡呢？

睡眠把她的手指放在大地的雙眼上。
鴉巢逐漸沉寂，竹葉的呢喃也默然無聲。

勞動的人們從田裡回到家中，在庭院裡鋪開席子。
市集已過，你在夜晚提著籃子匆忙的要到哪裡呢？

FIFTY-FOUR

Where do you hurry with your basket this late evening when the marketing is over?

They all have come home with their burdens; the moon peeps from above the village trees.

The echoes of the voices calling for the ferry run across the dark water to the distant swamp where wild ducks sleep.

Where do you hurry with your basket when the marketing is over?

Sleep has laid her fingers upon the eyes of the earth.

The nests of the crows have become silent, and the murmurs of the bamboo leaves are silent.

The labourers home from their fields spread their mats in the courtyards.

Where do you hurry with your basket when the marketing is over?

你離開的時候，是正午時分。

烈日當空。

當你離開的時候，我已經完成工作，獨自坐在陽台上。

不定的風吹來，含帶著許多遠野的氣息。

鴿子們在樹蔭下不知疲倦的咕咕叫著，有一隻蜜蜂在我的房中盤旋著，嗡嗡聲傳達著許多遠野的消息。

村莊在中午的炎熱中熟睡。道路橫在那裡，空寂無人。

樹葉沙沙，忽起忽落。

當村莊在中午的炎熱中熟睡的時候，我凝視著天空，把一個我知道的名字織進蔚藍中。

我忘記束起我的頭髮。慵懶的微風在我的臉頰上，與它一起嬉鬧。

河流在陰涼的河岸下，平靜的流淌著。

懶洋洋的白雲，一動也不動。

我忘記束起我的頭髮。

你離開的時候，是正午時分。

路上的塵土灼熱，田野在喘息著。

鴿子們在濃密的枝葉間，咕咕的叫著。

當你離開的時候，我獨自在陽台上。

FIFTY-FIVE

It was mid-day when you went away.

The sun was strong in the sky. I had done my work and sat alone on my balcony when you went away.

Fitful gusts came winnowing through the smells of many distant fields.

The doves cooed tireless in the shade, and a bee strayed in my room humming the news of many distant fields.

The village slept in the noonday heat. The road lay deserted.

In sudden fits the rustling of the leaves rose and died.

I gazed at the sky and wove in the blue the letters of a name I had known, while the village slept in the noonday heat.

I had forgotten to braid my hair. The languid breeze played with it upon my neck.

The river ran unruffled under the shady bank.

The lazy white clouds did not move.

I had forgotten to braid my hair.

It was mid-day when you went away.

The dust of the road was hot and the fields panting.

The doves cooed among the dense leaves.

I was alone in my balcony when you went away.

56

我是眾多忙於日常瑣碎家務的女人中的一個。

為什麼你單單選擇我，把我從日常生活的涼爽蔽蔭中帶出來？

尚未表達的愛是聖潔的。它像寶石一樣，隱藏在朦朧的心中閃閃發光。在奇異的日光中，它顯得可憐的晦暗。

啊，你打碎我的心蓋，把我顫抖的愛情拖到空曠的地方，永遠摧毀它藏身的幽暗巢穴的一角。

其他的女人永遠和從前一樣。

沒有一個人窺探到她們的內心深處，她們自己也不知道自己的秘密。

她們輕輕的微笑、哭泣、閒談、工作。她們每天去寺廟，點亮她們的燈，然後到河邊打水。

我希望可以從無遮掩的顫抖的羞愧中，把我的愛救出來，但是你轉頭不管。

是的，你的道路在你的面前延伸，但是你卻切斷我的歸路，把我赤裸裸的留在這個沒有眼瞼的眼睛日夜瞪視的世界前。

FIFTY-SIX

I was one among many women busy with the obscure daily tasks of the household.

Why did you single me out and bring me away from the cool shelter of our common life?

Love unexpressed is sacred. It shines like gems in the gloom of the hidden heart. In the light of the curious day it looks pitifully dark.

Ah, you broke through the cover of my heart and dragged my trembling love into the open place, destroying for ever the shady corner where it hid its nest.

The other women are the same as ever.

No one has peeped into their inmost being, and they themselves know not their own secret.

Lightly they smile, and weep, chatter, and work. Daily they go to the temple, light their lamps, and fetch water from the river.

I hope my love would be saved from the shivering shame of the shelterless, but you turn your face away.

Yes, your path lies open before you, but you have cut off my return, and left me stripped naked before the world with its lidless eyes staring night and day.

啊，世界，我採了你的花！

我把它貼在胸前，花兒刺痛我。

日光退卻，天色暗淡，我發現花兒已經凋謝，但是疼痛依舊。

啊，世界，有更多的花兒將會來到你這裡，帶著芳香，帶著驕傲！

但是，我的採花時間已經過去了，暗夜悠長，我沒有我的玫瑰，只有疼痛依舊。

FIFTY-SEVEN

I plucked your flower, O world!

I pressed it to my heart and the thorn pricked.

When the day waned and it darkened, I found that the flower had faded, but the pain remained.

More flowers will come to you with perfume and pride, O world!

But my time for flower-gathering is over, and through the dark night I have not my rose, only the pain remains.

在某一天清晨的花園中，有一個盲女獻給我一串用荷葉蓋著的花環。

我把它戴在頸上，淚水湧上我的雙眼。

我吻了她，說：「你簡直和花兒一樣的盲目。你自己不知道你的禮物是多麼的美麗。」

FIFTY-FIGHT

One morning in the flower garden a blind girl came to offer me a flower chain in the cover of a lotus leaf.

I put it round my neck, and tears came to my eyes.

I kissed her and said, "You are blind even as the flowers are. You yourself know not how beautiful is your gift."

　　女人啊，你不僅僅是上帝的手工藝品，也是男人的手工藝品；他們永遠從心中用美來裝扮你。

　　詩人用比喻的金絲線為你織網；畫家把永新的不朽贈給你的形體。

　　大海拿出珍珠，寶礦獻上黃金，夏天的花園獻上鮮花來裝扮你、覆蓋你，讓你更珍貴。

　　人們心中的渴望，在你的青春上，灑下它的輝煌。

　　你一半是女人，一半是夢幻。

FIFTY-NINE

O woman, you are not merely the handiwork of God, but also of men; these are ever endowing you with beauty from their hearts.

Poets are weaving for you a web with threads of golden imagery; painters are giving your form ever new immortality.

The sea gives its pearls, the mines their gold, the summer gardens their flowers to deck you, to cover you, to make you more precious.

The desire of men's hearts has shed its glory over your youth.

You are one half woman and one half dream.

在生命的奔騰怒吼中，噢，美麗被刻進石頭，你站著，靜默無言，孤獨漠然。

偉大的時間迷戀的坐在你的腳邊，低語：「說吧，對我說吧，我的愛人；說吧，我的新娘！」

但是，你的話語在石頭中封閉，噢，堅定不移的美麗！

SIXTY

Amidst the rush and roar of life, O Beauty, carved in stone, you stand mute and still, alone and aloof.

Great Time sits enamoured at your feet and murmurs: "Speak, speak to me, my love; speak, my bride!"

But your speech is shut up in stone, O Immovable Beauty!

安靜吧，我的心，讓離別的時刻甜美動人吧！

讓它不是死亡，而是圓滿。
讓愛融入記憶，讓痛苦融入歌曲。
讓穿越天空的飛翔，以歸巢斂翼作為結局。
讓你雙手的最後接觸，像夜晚中的花朵一樣溫柔。

靜默的站著，啊，美麗的結局，在靜默中說出你的最後的言辭。
我對你鞠躬，舉起我的燈，照亮你的歸途。

SIXTY-ONE

Peace, my heart, let the time for the parting be sweet.

Let it not be a death but completeness.
Let love melt into memory and pain into songs.
Let the flight through the sky end in the folding of the wings over the nest.
Let the last touch of your hands be gentle like the flower of the night.

Stand still, O Beautiful End, for a moment, and say your last words in silence.
I bow you and hold up my lamp to light you on your way.

62

在夢境的幽暗小路上，我追尋著我的前世愛戀。

她的房子站立在荒涼的街道盡頭。

在夜晚的微風中，她寵愛的孔雀在架上昏睡，鴿子在牠們的角落裡沉默著。

她把燈放在門邊，站在我的面前。

她抬起一雙大眼睛望著我的臉，無聲的問：「你好嗎，我的朋友？」

我試圖回答，但是我們的語言卻已經迷失和忘卻。

我想了又想，卻怎麼也想不起我們的名字。

淚水在她的眼中閃爍。她向我伸出右手。我拉著她的手，默默的站著。

我們的燈在夜晚的微風中，搖曳著熄滅了。

SIXTY-TWO

In the dusky path of a dream I went to seek the love who was mine in a former life.

Her house stood at the end of a desolate street.
In the evening breeze her pet peacock sat drowsing on its perch, and the pigeons were silent in their corner.

She set her lamp down by the portal and stood before me.
She raised her large eyes to my face and mutely asked, "Are you well, my friend?"

I tried to answer, but our language had been lost and forgotten.
I thought and thought; our names would not come to my mind.

Tears shone in her eyes. She held up her right hand to me. I took it and stood silent.
Our lamp had flickered in the evening breeze and died.

旅人，你必須走嗎？

夜靜靜的，黑暗在森林上酣睡。

我們的陽台上燈光明亮，花兒全都新鮮嬌豔，年輕的眼睛仍然清醒著。

你離開的時間到了嗎？

旅人，你必須走嗎？

我們不曾用懇求的手臂來束縛你的雙足。

你的門開著。你的馬已經備好鞍韉，站在門口。

如果我們試圖擋住你的去路，那只能用我們的歌曲。

如果我們曾經想挽留你，那只能用我們的眼睛。

旅人，我們沒有希望留住你。我們有的只是淚水。

是怎樣不滅的火光，在你的眼中閃耀？

是怎樣不平的狂熱，在你的血液中奔騰？

是怎樣的呼喚，在黑暗中催促你？

你在天上的星星中，讀到的是怎樣可怕的咒語，帶著封存的秘密消息，在黑夜靜默而怪異的進入你的心中的時候？

如果你不在意歡樂的聚會，如果你必須擁有寧靜而疲憊的心啊，我們就熄滅燈火，停止琴聲。

我們將會靜靜的坐在樹葉沙沙的黑暗裡，疲倦的月亮將會在你的窗上，灑下慘白的光輝。

旅人啊，是怎樣不眠的精靈，從午夜的心中與你接觸？

SIXTY-THREE

Traveller, must you go?

The night is still and the darkness swoons upon the forest.

The lamps are bright in our balcony, the flowers all fresh, and the youthful eyes still awake.

Is the time for your parting come?

Traveller, must you go?

We have not bound your feet with our entreating arms.

Your doors are open. Your horse stands saddled at the gate.

If we have tried to bar your passage it was but with our songs.

Did we ever try to hold you back it was but with our eyes.

Traveller, we are helpless to keep you. We have only our tears.

What quenchless fire glows in your eyes?

What restless fever runs in your blood?

What call from the dark urges you?

What awful incantation have you read among the stars in the sky, that with a sealed secret message the night entered your heart, silent and strange?

If you do not care for merry meetings, if you must have peace, weary heart, we shall put our lamps out and silence our harps.

We shall sit still in the dark in the rustle of leaves, and the tired moon will shed pale rays on your window.

O traveller, what sleepless spirit has touched you from the heart of the midnight?

我在路上灼熱的塵土上，度過我的白晝。

現在，在夜晚的涼爽中，我敲響一家客棧的門。它已經被廢棄，淪為一片廢墟。

一棵冷酷的菩提樹，從牆垣的裂隙裡，伸出饑餓的爪根。

曾經，有路人來這裡清洗他們疲累的雙足。

在新月暗淡的清光中，他們在庭院裡鋪開席子，坐著談論陌生的國度。

清晨，他們精神煥發，鳥兒讓他們歡悅，友善的花朵在路邊向他們點著頭。

但是，當我來到這裡的時候，卻沒有點燃的燈在等待我。

許多被遺忘的夜燈所留下的薰黑煙垢，像盲人的眼睛，從牆上瞪視著我。

螢火蟲在乾涸的池塘附近的草叢裡閃爍，竹影在青草蔓生的小徑上搖曳。

我是白晝盡頭的沒有主人的孤客。

漫漫長夜落在我的面前，我累了。

SIXTY-FOUR

I spent my day on the scorching hot dust of the road.

Now, in the cool of the evening, I knock at the door of the inn. It is deserted and in ruins.

A grim ashath tree spreads its hungry clutching roots through the gaping fissures of the walks.

Days have been when wayfarers came here to wash their weary feet.

They spread their mats in the courtyard in the dim light of the early moon, and sat and talked of strange lands.

They woke refreshed in the morning when birds made them glad, and friendly flowers nodded their heads at them from the wayside.

But no lighted lamp awaited me when I came here.

The black smudges of smoke left by many a forgotten evening lamp stare, like blind eyes, from the wall.

Fireflies flit in the bush near the dried-up pond, and bamboo branches fling their shadows on the grass-grown path.

I am the guest of no one at the end of my day.

The long night is before me, and I am tired.

那又是你的呼喚嗎？

夜晚來臨了。疲憊像求愛的手臂一樣，緊緊的箍著我。

你在呼喚我嗎？

我已經把我的所有白晝都給你，殘忍的情人啊，難道你一定還要掠奪我的夜晚嗎？

萬事終將有盡頭，黑暗中的幽靜，是屬於一個人的。

難道你的聲音一定要穿透它來刺激我嗎？

難道你的門前的夜晚沒有催眠曲嗎？

難道那個生著靜默之翼的星星，從未爬上你的無情之塔的天空嗎？

難道你的花園中的花朵，從未在溫柔的死亡中跌落塵埃嗎？

難道你一定要呼喚我嗎，你這個不安份的人？

那就讓愛的憂傷的眼睛，徒然的因為凝望而哭泣。

讓燈盞在孤寂的房中燃燒。

讓渡船把疲憊的工人載回家。

我把夢幻丟在身後，奔向你的呼喚。

SIXTY-FIVE

Is that your call again?

The evening has come. Weariness clings around me like the arms of entreating love.

Do you call me?

I had given all my day to you, cruel mistress, must you also rob me of my night?

Somewhere there is an end to everything, and the loneness of the dark is one's own.

Must your voice cut through it and smite me?

Has the evening no music of sleep at your gate?

Do the silent-winged stars never climb the sky above your pitiless tower?

Do the flowers never drop on the dust in soft death in your garden?

Must you call me, you unquiet one?

Then let the sad eyes of love vainly watch and weep.

Let the lamp burn in the lonely house.

Let the ferry-boat take the weary labourers to their home.

I leave behind my dreams and I hasten to your call.

66

　　一個流浪的瘋子，在尋找點金石。他的褐色頭髮蓬亂的黏滿泥土，身形瘦得像一個影子，緊閉的雙唇，像緊閉的心扉，他的燒灼的眼睛，就像在尋找伴侶的螢火蟲的燈火。

　　在他的面前，是咆哮的無邊海洋。
　　喧鬧的海浪，不停的談論著隱藏的珍寶，嘲笑著不知道它們的意義的無知之徒。

　　或許他現在已經不存希望，但是他不會休息，因為搜尋已經成為他的生命——
　　就像那海洋，永遠向天空伸舉著手臂，乞求著不可企及的東西——
　　就像那星辰，循環往復，卻是追尋一個永遠無法達到的目標——

　　瘋子的褐色頭髮蓬亂的黏滿泥土，他仍然在孤寂的海岸上遊蕩，搜尋他的點金石。

SIXTY-SIX

A wandering madman was seeking the touchstone, with matted locks, tawny and dust-laden, and body worn to a shadow, his lips tight-pressed, like the shut-up doors of his heart, his burning eyes like the lamp of a glow-worm seeking its mate.

Before him the endless ocean roared.
The garrulous waves ceaselessly talked of hidden treasures, mocking the ignorance that knew not their meaning.

Maybe he now had no hope remaining, yet he would not rest, for the search had become his life,——
Just as the ocean for ever lifts its arms to the sky for the unattainable ——
Just as the stars go in circles, yet seeking a goal that can never be reached ——

Even so on the lonely shore the madman with dusty tawny locks still roamed in search of the touchstone.

有一天，一個村童走過來，問：「告訴我，你腰上的那一條金鏈是從哪裡來的？」

　　瘋子驚跳起來——那一條原本是鐵的鏈子，卻已經變成黃金；這不是一場夢，但是他不知道變化是何時發生的。

　　他狂亂的敲著自己的前額——哪裡，啊，在哪裡不知不覺的竟然成功了？

　　撿起石頭，碰碰鏈子，再把它們扔掉，不看看是否發生變化；就這樣，已經養成習慣，瘋子找到點金石，又失去點金石。

　　太陽西沉，天空一片金黃。

　　瘋子沿著自己的腳印返回，重新尋找丟失的珍寶。他的力量耗盡了，身體彎曲了，他的心在塵土中枯萎，像一棵連根拔起的樹。

One day a village boy came up and asked, "Tell me, where did you come at this golden chain about your waist?"

The madman started——the chain that once was iron was verily gold; it was not a dream, but he did not know when it had changed.

He struck his forehead wildly —— where, O where had he without knowing it achieved success?

It had grown into a habit, to pick up pebbles and touch the chain, and to throw them away without looking to see if a change had come; thus the madman found and lost the touchstone.

The sun was sinking low in the west, the sky was of gold.

The madman returned on his footsteps to seek anew the lost treasure, with his strength gone, his body bent, and his heart in the dust, like a tree uprooted.

雖然夜晚緩步來臨，宣告一切歌聲的停息；
雖然你的夥伴都去休息，你也疲倦了；
雖然恐怖在黑暗中瀰漫，天空的臉也被遮掩；
但是，鳥兒，我的鳥兒啊，請聽我說，不要收起你的翅膀。

這不是森林中的樹葉的陰影，這是大海像一條深黑的蛇一樣在漲溢。
這不是盛開的茉莉花的舞蹈，這是泡沫在閃耀。
啊，哪裡是明媚青碧的海岸，哪裡是你的巢穴？

鳥兒，我的鳥兒啊，請聽我說，不要收起你的翅膀。
孤獨的夜晚躺在你的小路上，黎明在幽暗群山的背後酣眠。
星辰屏住呼吸計算著時間，柔弱的月兒在深深的夜色中遊蕩。

鳥兒，我的鳥兒啊，請聽我說，不要收起你的翅膀。
對於你，這裡沒有希望，沒有恐懼。
這裡沒有言辭，沒有私語，沒有哭喊。
這裡沒有家，沒有休息的床。
這裡只有你自己的一雙翅膀和一片茫茫無徑的天空。
鳥兒，我的鳥兒啊，請聽我說，不要收起你的翅膀。

SIXTY-SEVEN

Though the evening comes with slow steps and has signalled for all songs to cease;

Though your companions have gone to their rest and you are tired;

Though fear broods in the dark and the face of the sky is veiled;

Yet, bird, O my bird, listen to me, do not close your wings.

That is not the gloom of the leaves of the forest, that is the sea swelling like a dark black snake.

That is not the dance of the flowering jasmine, that is flashing foam.

Ah, where is the sunny green shore, where is your nest?

Bird, O my bird, listen to me, do not close your wings.

The lone night lies along your path, the dawn sleeps behind the shadowy hills.

The stars hold their breath counting the hours, the feeble moon swims the deep night.

Bird, O my bird, listen to me, do not close your wings.

There is no hope, no fear for you.

There is no word, no whisper, no cry.

There is no home, no bed of rest.

There is only your own pair of wings and the pathless sky.

Bird, O my bird, listen to me, do not close your wings.

68

　　沒有人會永遠活著，兄弟，也沒有什麼東西會長久存在。把這個記在心中，高興起來吧！

　　我們的生命不是陳舊的負擔，我們的道路不是漫長的旅程。
　　一個孤單的詩人，不必去唱一首古老的歌謠。
　　花朵枯萎凋謝，但是戴花的人不必為它永遠哀傷。
　　兄弟，把這個記在心中，高興起來吧！

　　想要把完美編進樂曲，必須有一個完整的休止符。
　　為了沉浸於輝煌的金影，生命向它的日落滑入。
　　想要從遊戲中把愛召回，必須啜飲悲痛，並且降生於淚水的天堂。
　　兄弟，把這個記在心中，高興起來吧！

　　我們匆匆的採集花朵，唯恐它們被路過的風兒掠走。
　　奪取稍縱即逝的熱吻，讓我們熱血沸騰，目光炯炯。
　　我們的生命是熱切的，我們的渴望是強烈的，因為時間在鳴奏著離別之鐘。
　　兄弟，把這個記在心中，高興起來吧！

SIXTY-EIGHT

None lives for ever, brother, and nothing lasts for long. Keep that in mind and rejoice.

Our life is not the one old burden, our path is not the one long journey.
One sole poet has not to sing one aged song.
The flower fades and dies; but he who wears the flower has not to mourn for it for ever.
Brother, keep that in mind and rejoice.

There must come a full pause to weave perfection into music.
Life droops toward its sunset to be drowned in the golden shadows.
Love must be called from its play to drink sorrow and be borne to the heaven of tears.
Brother, keep that in mind and rejoice.

We hasten to gather our flowers lest they are plundered by the passing winds.
It quickens our blood and brightens our eyes to snatch kisses that would vanish if we delayed.
Our life is eager, our desires are keen, for time tolls the bell of parting.
Brother, keep that in mind and rejoice.

我們沒有時間去握緊一件東西，把它壓碎以後，再棄於塵土中。

　　時間匆匆走過，把夢幻都藏在裙底。

　　我們的生命短暫，只有幾天分給愛戀。

　　如果是為了工作和勞役，生命就會變得無盡漫長。

　　兄弟，把這個記在心中，高興起來吧！

　　美對我們是甜蜜的，因為她與我們的生命伴隨著同樣短暫的旋律起舞。

　　知識對我們是寶貴的，因為我們永遠沒有時間去完成它。

　　所有的一切，都在永久的天堂裡完成。

　　但是，大地上幻想的花朵，卻被死亡保存得清新鮮豔。

　　兄弟，把這個記在心中，高興起來吧！

There is not time for us to clasp a thing and crush it and fling it away to the dust.

The hours trip rapidly away, hiding their dreams in their skirts.

Our life is short; it yields but a few days for love.

Were it for work and drudgery it would be endlessly long.

Brother, keep that in mind and rejoice.

Beauty is sweet to us, because she dances to the same fleeting tune with our lives.

Knowledge is precious to us, because we shall never have time to complete it.

All is done and finished in the eternal Heaven.

But earth's flowers of illusion are kept eternally fresh by death.

Brother, keep that in mind and rejoice.

　　我要獵取那隻金鹿。

　　或許你會笑，我的朋友，但是我要追趕那個躲避我的幻想。

　　我奔越過山岡峽谷，我穿行過無名的國土，因為我在獵取那隻金鹿。

　　你到市集採購，又滿載著貨物回家，但是我不知道何時何地一陣無家之風碰觸到我。

　　我的心中沒有牽掛；一切的所有，都被我遠遠的拋在身後。

　　我奔越過山岡峽谷，我穿行過無名的國土，因為我在獵取那隻金鹿。

SIXTY-NINE

I hunt for the golden stag.

You may smile, my friends, but I pursue the vision that eludes me.
I run across hills and dales, I wander through nameless lands,
because I am hunting for the golden stag.

You come and buy in the market and go back to your homes laden
with goods, but the spell of the homeless winds has touched me I
know not when and where.

I have no care in my heart; all my belongings I have left far behind me.
I run across hills and dales, I wander through nameless lands —
— because I am hunting for the golden stag.

記得在我兒時，有一天，我曾經把一隻紙船放進溝渠裡。
那是七月的一個潮濕的日子，我獨自高興的沉浸在自己的遊戲中。

我把我的紙船放進溝渠裡。
忽然，烏雲密佈，狂風怒吼，暴雨傾注。
混濁的流水奔湧翻騰，淹沒我的紙船。

我心裡難過的想，暴風雨是故意來破壞我的歡樂；它的一切惡意，都是針對我。

今天，七月的陰天是漫長的，我在回想著在我的生命中以我為失敗者的一切遊戲。
我責怪命運對我百般嘲弄，忽然，我想起那隻沉在溝渠裡的紙船。

SEVENTY

I remember a day in my childhood I floated a paper boat in the ditch.

It was a wet of July; I was alone and happy over my play.

I floated my paper boat in the ditch.

Suddenly the storm clouds thickened, winds came in gusts, and rain poured in torrents.

Rills of muddy water rushed and swelled the stream and sunk my boat.

Bitterly I thought in my mind that the storm came on purpose to spoil my happiness; all its malice was against me.

The cloudy day of July is long today, and I have been musing over all those games in life wherein I was loser.

I was blaming my fate for the many tricks it played on me, when suddenly I remembered the paper boat that sank in the ditch.

白天還沒有結束，市集也沒有散去——河岸上的市集。

我曾經擔心我的時間被耗盡，我的最後一分錢也失去了。

但是，沒有，我的兄弟，我還剩下一些東西。我的命運沒有把我的一切都騙走。

買與賣都結束了。

雙方的稅款都已經繳齊，我應該回家了。

但是，守門人，你要你的通行費嗎？

不要害怕，我還剩下一些東西。我的命運沒有把我的一切都騙走。

風中的間歇，預示著暴雨；西方低垂的陰雲，預報著噩兆。

安靜的水面，等待著狂風。

在黑夜襲擊我之前，我趕緊渡河。

哦，擺渡者，你要你的酬金！

是的，兄弟，我還剩下一些東西。我的命運沒有把我的一切都騙走。

SEVENTY-ONE

The day is not yet done, the fair is not over, the fair on the river-bank.

I had feared that my time had been squandered and my last penny lost.

But no, my brother, I have still something left. My fate has not cheated me of everything.

The selling and buying are over.

All the dues on both sides have been gathered in, and it is time for me to go home.

But, gatekeeper, do you ask for your toll?

Do not fear, I have still something left. My fate has not cheated me of everything.

The lull in the wind threatens storm, and the lowering clouds in the west bode no good.

The hushed water waits for the wind.

I hurry to cross the river before the night overtakes me.

O ferryman, you want your fee!

Yes, brother, I have still something left. My fate has not cheated me of everything.

路邊的樹下，坐著一個乞丐。天啊，他懷著膽怯的希望，看著我的臉！

　　他認為我富足的攜帶著一天的利潤。

　　是的，兄弟，我還剩下一些東西。我的命運沒有把我的一切都騙走。

　　夜色變濃了，道路很孤寂。螢火蟲在枝葉間閃爍。

　　是誰以悄悄的躡步在跟著我？

　　啊，我知道了，你想掠奪我的所有收穫。我不會讓你失望！

　　因為，我還剩下一些東西，我的命運沒有把我的一切都騙走。

　　半夜，我到家了，兩手空空。

　　你正在門口等著我，滿眼焦急，毫無睡意，沉默不語。

　　你像一隻膽怯的鳥，帶著熱烈的愛意，飛向我的懷抱。

　　唉，唉，我的上帝，我還有許多剩餘！我的命運沒有把我的一切都騙走。

In the wayside under the tree sits the beggar. Alas, he looks at my face with a timid hope!

He thinks I am rich with the day's profit.

Yes, brother, I have still something left. My fate has not cheated me for everything.

The night grows dark and the road lonely. Fireflies gleam among the leaves.

Who are you that follow me with stealthy silent steps?

Ah, I know, it is your desire to rob me of all my gains. I will not disappoint you!

For I still have something left, and my fate has not cheated me of everything.

At midnight I reach home. My hands are empty.

You are waiting with anxious eyes at my door, sleepless and silent.

Like a timorous bird you fly to my breast with eager love.

Ay, ay, my God, much remains still. My fate has not cheated me of everything.

經過幾天的辛苦工作，我建起一座廟宇。它沒有門，也沒有窗，牆壁用厚重的巨石層層疊起。

我忘記其他的一切，我避開整個世界，我凝神注視著被我放在神龕裡的聖像。

裡面總是黑夜，以芳香的油燈來照明。

連綿而薰香的煙霧，把我的心纏繞在它的厚重的漩渦裡。

我沒有睡意，用迷亂的線條在牆上刻畫出一些奇異的形象——生翼的馬兒，人面的花兒，肢體如蛇的女人。

我不在任何地方留下通道，讓鳥兒的歌聲、樹葉的呢喃、村鎮的喧囂得以進入。

在黑暗的穹頂上，唯一的聲音是我唱經的回響。

我的思想變得敏銳而篤定，像一個犀利的光焰，我的感覺在狂喜中陶醉。

我不知道時間怎樣流逝，直到巨雷劈開這座廟宇，一陣劇痛刺穿我的心。

燈火看起來蒼白而怯懦；牆上的刻痕像是被封鎖的夢，在光線中眼神迷離的呆望著，好像要把自己藏起來。

我看著神龕裡的聖像。我看到它在上帝的鮮活觸摸下，微笑了，活著了。被我囚禁的黑夜，展翅飛逝了。

SEVENTY-TWO

With days of hard travail I raised a temple. It had no doors or windows, its walls were thickly built with massive stones.

I forgot all else, I shunned all the world, I gazed in rapt contemplation at the image I had set upon the altar.

It was always night inside, and lit by the lamps of perfumed oil.

The ceaseless smoke of incense wound my heart in its heavy coils.

Sleepless, I carved on the walls fantastic figures in mazy bewildering lines —— winged horses, flowers with human faces, women with limbs like serpents.

No passage was left anywhere through which could enter the song of birds, the murmur of leaves or hum of the busy village.

The only sound that echoed in its dark dome was that of incantations which I chanted.

My mind became keen and still like a pointed flame, my senses swooned in ecstasy.

I knew not how time passed till the thunderstone had struck the temple, and a pain stung me through the heart.

The lamp looked pale and ashamed; the carvings on the walls, like chained dreams, stared meaningless in the light as they would fain hide themselves.

I looked at the image on the altar. I saw it smiling and alive with the living touch of God. The night I had imprisoned had spread its wings and vanished.

無限的財富不屬於你，我的堅忍的、微黑的塵埃之母！

你奔波著去填滿你的孩子的嘴，但是食物卻很少。

你給我們的歡樂贈禮，從來就不完美。

你為孩子們做的玩具，是脆弱的。

你不能滿足我們全部的迫切願望，但是我應該因此而背棄你嗎？

你的含著痛苦陰影的微笑，在我的眼中是多麼的甜美。

你的永無止境的愛，在我的心中是多麼的珍貴。

從你的乳房中，你哺育我們，用的是生命，而非永恆，因此你的眼睛永遠是清醒的。

世世代代，你用色彩與詩歌來工作，但是你的天堂尚未建起，僅有一些哀傷的痕跡。

你的美的創造，蒙著淚水的迷霧。

我將會把我的詩歌傾入你的靜默的心裡，把我的愛傾入你的愛之中。

我將會用工作來膜拜你。

我見過你的和藹的臉龐，我愛你的悲苦的塵土，大地母親。

SEVENTY-THREE

Infinite wealth is not yours, my patient and dusky mother dust!
You toil to fill the mouths of your children, but food is scarce.
The gift of gladness that you have for us is never perfect.
The toys that you make for your children are fragile.
You cannot satisfy all our hungry hopes, but should I desert you
for that?

Your smile which is shadowed with pain is sweet to my eyes.
Your love which knows not fulfilment is dear to my heart.

From your breast you have fed us with life but not immortality,
that is why your eyes are ever wakeful.
For ages you are working with colour and song, yet your heaven
is not built, but only its sad suggestion.

Over your creations of beauty there is the mist of tears.

I will pour my songs into your mute heart, and my love into your
love.
I will worship you with labour.

I have seen your tender face and I love your mournful dust,
Mother Earth.

在世界的觀眾大廳裡，一片單純的草葉，與陽光和午夜的
星辰一起，坐在同一條地毯上。

就這樣，我的詩歌，在世界的心房裡，與雲彩和森林的音
樂一起，分享它們的席位。
但是，你這個富人，在太陽的歡樂金光中，在月亮的沉思
柔光中，這些單純的輝煌，你的財富卻不佔分毫。

擁抱萬物的天空灑下的祝福，並沒有落到它的身上。
當死神出現的時候，它會蒼白枯萎，碎為泥塵。

SEVENTY-FOUR

In the world's audience hall, the simple blade of grass sits on the same carpet with the sunbeam and the stars of midnight.

Thus my songs share their seats in the heart of the world with the music of the clouds and forests.

But, you man of riches, your wealth has no part in the simple grandeur of the sun's glad gold and the mellow gleam of the musing moon.

The blessing of all-embracing sky is not shed upon it.

And when death appears, it pales and withers and crumbles into dust.

　　午夜，那個想做苦行僧的人宣告：「捨家求神的時候到了。啊，是誰讓我在這裡迷戀這麼久呢？」

　　上帝低語道：「我。」但是這個人的耳朵是塞住的。

　　他的妻子抱著熟睡的嬰兒，安靜的睡在床的一邊。

　　那個人說：「你是誰，愚弄了我這麼久？」

　　那個聲音又說道：「他們是上帝。」但是他沒有聽到。

　　嬰兒在睡夢中哭了，靠向母親。

　　上帝命令道：「停下來吧，傻瓜，不要離開你的家。」但是他仍然沒有聽到。

　　上帝嘆了一口氣，抱怨道：「為什麼我的僕人要把我拋棄，卻又到處尋找我呢？」

SEVENTY-FIVE

At midnight the would-be ascetic announced: "This is the time to give up my home and seek for God. Ah, who has held me so long in delusion here?"

God whispered, "I," but the ears of the man were stopped.

With a baby asleep at her breast lay his wife, peacefully sleeping on one side of the bed.

The man said, "Who are you that have fooled me so long?"

The voice said again, "They are God," but he heard it not.

The baby cried out in its dream, nestling close to its mother.

God commanded, "Stop, fool, leave not thy home," but still he heart not.

God sighed and complained, "Why does my servant wander to seek me, forsaking me?"

市集在寺廟前進行著。

一大早就開始下雨了，白天就要結束了。

比群眾的所有喜悅更明麗的，是一個小姑娘的燦爛微笑，她花一分錢買到一個棕櫚葉哨子。

清脆歡樂的哨聲，飄蕩在一切的笑聲與喧嘩之上。

不見盡頭的群眾，熙熙攘攘。道路泥濘，河水流溢，田地浸潤在連續不斷的雨水裡。

比群眾的所有煩惱更惱人的，是一個小男孩的煩惱——他想買一根彩棒，卻沒有一分錢。

他的渴求的眼睛盯著那間小店，讓整個成人的聚會，變成如此的令人同情。

SEVENTY-SIX

The fair was on before the temple.
It had rained from the early morning and the day came to its end.

Brighter than all the gladness of the crowd was the bright smile of
a girl who bought for a farthing a whistle of palm leaf.
The shrill joy of that whistle floated above all laughter and noise.

An endless throng of people came and jostled together. The road
was muddy, the river in flood, the field under water in ceaseless rain.

Greater than all the troubles of the crowd was a little boy's
trouble —— he had not a farthing to buy a painted stick.
His wistful eyes gazing at the shop made this whole meeting of
men so pitiful.

村西來的工人和他的妻子，正在忙著為磚窯挖土。

他們的小女兒到河邊的渡頭上；在那裡，她無休無止的洗著鍋碗瓢盆。

她的小弟弟，剃著光頭，赤裸的身體被曬得黑黑的，黏滿泥漿，緊緊的跟著她，聽話的在高高的河岸上，耐心的等待。

她頂著滿滿的水瓶，左手拎著發亮的銅壺，右手拉著小弟弟，走回家中——她是媽媽的小僕人，繁重的家務讓她變得嚴肅。

有一天，我看見這個赤裸的小男孩伸著腿坐著。

他的姐姐坐在水中，用一把泥土轉來轉去的擦洗著水壺。

在附近，有一隻毛茸茸的小羊，站在河岸上吃草。

牠走近小男孩坐著的地方，忽然扯開嗓子大叫，小男孩被嚇得哭喊起來。

他的姐姐放下手中清洗的東西，跑上岸來。

她一手抱起弟弟，一手抱起小羊，把她的愛撫分成兩半；人類的孩子和動物的孩子，在慈愛的連結中，合而為一。

SEVENTY-SEVEN

The workman and his wife from the west country are busy digging to make bricks of the kiln.

Their little daughter goes to the landing-place by the river; there she has no end of scouring and scrubbing of pots and pans.

Her littler brother, with shaven head and brown, naked, mud-covered limbs, follows after her and waits patiently on the high bank at her bidding.

She goes back home with the full pitcher poised on her head, the shining brass pot in her left hand, holding the child with her right—— she the tiny servant of her mother, grave with the weight of the household cares.

One day I saw this naked boy sitting with legs outstretched.

In the water his sister sat rubbing a drinking-pot with a handful of earth, turning it round and round.

Near by a soft-haired lamb stood gazing along the bank.

It came close to where the boy sat and suddenly bleated aloud, and the child started up and screamed.

His sister left off cleaning her pot and ran up.

She took up her brother in one arm and the lamb in the other, and dividing her caresses between them bound in one bond of affection the offspring of beast and man.

　　那是在五月裡。悶熱的中午，似乎無盡的漫長。在熱浪中，乾燥的大地渴得張著口。

　　此時，我聽到有一個聲音在河邊叫道：「過來吧，親愛的！」

　　我闔上書，打開窗戶，向外望去。

　　我看見一頭大水牛，身上黏著泥漿，站在小河附近，眼中全是寧靜與忍耐；有一個年輕人，站在及膝深的水中，呼喚牠去洗澡。

　　我高興的笑了，心裡感到一陣甜蜜的感動。

SEVENTY-EIGHT

It was in May. The sultry noon seemed endlessly long. The dry earth gaped with thirst in the heat.

When I heard from the riverside a voice calling, "Come, my darling!"

I shut my book and opened the window to look out.

I saw a big buffalo with mud-stained hide, standing near the river with placid, patient eyes; and a youth, knee deep in water, calling it to its bath.

I smiled amused and felt a touch of sweetness in my heart.

　　我經常思考，人類和動物之間沒有語言，他們心中相通相知的界限在哪裡。

　　在一個遙遠的創世紀的清晨，他們的心穿過怎樣的太初樂園的清淺小徑，互相拜望。

　　他們的持續不變的足跡並未被抹掉，儘管他們的血緣關係早已被忘卻。

　　突然之間，在某一陣無言的樂聲中，那個模糊的記憶甦醒了，動物用溫柔的信任凝視著人類的臉龐，人類也用愉悅的友愛俯視著它的眼睛。

　　好像兩個朋友戴著面具相逢，透過偽裝，他們隱約的認識彼此。

SEVENTY-NINE

I often wonder where lie hidden the boundaries of recognition between man and the beast whose heart knows no spoken language.

Through what primal paradise in a remote morning of creation ran the simple path by which their hearts visited each other.

Those marks of their constant tread have not been effaced though their kinship has been long forgotten.

Yet suddenly in some wordless music the dim memory wakes up and the beast gazes into the man's face with a tender trust, and the man looks down into its eyes with amused affection.

It seems that the two friends meet masked and vaguely know each other through the disguise.

你秋波一瞥，就可以從詩人的豎琴上，掠走所有歌曲的財富，美麗的女人！

但是，你卻無心聽他們讚揚，因此我來讚頌你。

你可以讓世界上最高傲的頭在你的腳下伏倒。

但是，被你所崇拜、所鍾愛的是沒有名望的人，因此我崇拜你。

你的雙臂的完美觸摸，為帝王的輝煌增添榮耀。

但是，你卻用它們拂去塵土，拭淨你的卑微的家，因此我對你滿含敬畏。

EIGHTY

With a glance of your eyes you could plunder all the wealth of songs struck from poets' harps, fair woman!

But for their praises you have no ear, therefore I come to praise you.

You could humble at your feet the proudest heads in the world.

But it is your loved ones, unknown to fame, whom you choose to worship, therefore I worship you.

The perfection of your arms would add glory to kingly splendour with their touch.

But you use them to sweep away the dust, and to make clean your humble home, therefore I am filled with awe.

　　你為什麼這麼低聲的對我耳語，死神啊，我的死神？

　　當花兒在夜晚凋零，牛羊回到畜欄的時候，你悄悄的來到我的身邊，訴說著我聽不懂的語言。

　　難道你必須用昏睡的低語和冷酷的接吻來向我求愛、贏得我心嗎？死神啊，死神！

　　我們的婚禮，難道不會有盛大的儀式嗎？

　　你難道不會在你的茶色鬢髮上，繫上一個花環嗎？

　　難道沒有人會在你的面前打著旗幟？難道夜晚不會被你的火炬般的紅光燒亮嗎？死神啊，死神！

　　吹著你的海螺來吧，在無眠的夜晚來吧！

　　給我穿上紅豔的披風，抓緊我的手，把我帶走吧！

　　在我的門口備好你的車，讓你的馬兒們焦躁的嘶鳴吧！

　　揭開我的面紗，驕傲的看著我的臉吧，死神啊，我的死神！

EIGHTY-ONE

Why do you whisper so faintly in my ears, O Death, my Death?

When the flowers droop in the evening and cattle come back to their stalls, you stealthily come to my side and speak words that I do not understand.

Is this how you must woo and win me with the opiate of drowsy murmur and cold kisses, O Death, my Death?

Will there be no proud ceremony for our wedding?

Will you not tie up with a wreath your tawny coiled locks?

Is there none to carry your banner before you, and will not the night be on fire with your red torch-lights, O Death, my Death?

Come with your conch-shells sounding, come in the sleepless night.

Dress me with a crimson mantle, grasp my hand and take me.

Let your chariot be ready at my door with your horses neighing impatiently.

Raise my veil and look at my face proudly, O Death, my Death!

我和我的新娘，今晚要玩死亡的遊戲。

夜色漆黑，天空的雲起伏變幻，大海的波濤翻騰咆哮。
我和我的新娘，離開睡夢的暖榻，撞開門，衝了出去。
我們坐在鞦韆上，狂風從我們的身後，狠命的一推。
我的新娘嚇得又驚又喜，她顫抖著，緊緊的依偎在我的胸
前。
我溫柔的安撫她很久。
我為她鋪開花床，我關上房門，不讓強烈的光線照在她的
眼睛上。
我輕吻她的雙唇，溫柔的在她的耳畔低語，直到她酥軟的
半醒半睡。

她迷失在朦朧甜蜜而無邊無際的輕霧裡。
她對我的愛撫沒有回應，我的歌聲不能把她喚醒。

今夜，風暴的呼喚從曠野中來到。
我的新娘顫抖著站起來，她緊緊的抓著我的手，走出來。
她的頭髮在風中飛舞，她的面紗在臉上飄揚，她的花環在
胸前簌簌作響。

死亡的推力，把她推進生命中。
我和我的新娘，面對著面，心貼著心。

EIGHTY-TWO

We are to play the game of death tonight, my bride and I.

The night is black, the clouds in the sky are capricious, and the waves are raving at sea.

We have left our bed of dreams, flung open the door and come out, my bride and I.

We sit upon a swing, and the storm winds give us a wild push from behind.

My bride starts up with fear and delight, she trembles and clings to my breast.

Long have I served her tenderly.

I made for her a bed of flowers and I closed the doors to shut out the rude light from her eyes.

I kissed her gently on her lips and whispered softly in her ears till she half swooned in languor.

She was lost in the endless mist of vague sweetness.

She answered not to my touch, my songs failed to arouse her.

Tonight has come to us the call of the storm from the wild.

My bride has shivered and stood up, she has clasped my hand and come out.

Her hair is flying in the wind, her veil is fluttering, her garland rustles over her breast.

The push of death has swung her into life.

We are face to face and heart to heart, my bride and I.

　　她住在玉米田邊的山坡上，靠近那股嬉笑著流過古樹的莊嚴的陰影的清泉。女人們會到這裡注滿她們的水罐，旅人們會到這裡休息談話。她每天伴隨著泉水的潺潺韻律而工作與做夢。

　　有一天晚上，一個陌生人從白雲遮掩的山峰上走下來。他的頭髮像昏睡的蛇一樣，亂紛紛的糾纏著。我們驚奇的問：「你是誰？」他沒有回答，只是坐在喧鬧的水邊，默默的注視著她的茅屋。我們害怕得心裡亂跳，天黑的時候，我們都回家了。

　　第二天早晨，女人們到雪松旁的泉邊汲水，她們發現她的房門開著，但是，沒有她的聲音，她的笑臉在哪裡呢？

　　空空的水罐躺在地板上，她的牆角的燈早已燃盡熄滅。沒有人知道她在天亮前逃到哪裡了——那個陌生人也不見了。

EIGHTY-THREE

She dwelt on the hillside by the edge of a maize-field, near the spring that flows in laughing rills through the solemn shadows of ancient trees. The women came there to fill their jars, and travellers would sit there to rest and talk. She worked and dreamed daily to the tune of the bubbling stream.

One evening the stranger came down from the cloud-hidden peak; his locks were tangled like drowsy snakes. We asked in wonder, "Who are you?" He answered not but sat by the garrulous stream and silently gazed at the hut where she dwelt. Our hearts quaked in fear and we came back home when it was night.

Next morning when the women came to fetch water at the spring by the deodar trees, they found the doors open in her hut, but her voice was gone and where was her smiling face?

The empty jar lay on the floor and her lamp had burnt itself out in the corner. No one knew where she had fled to before it was morning —— and the stranger had gone.

五月，陽光漸強，積雪化盡，我們坐在泉邊哭泣。我們心中充滿懷疑：「她去的那片土地上有泉水嗎，在這些炎熱乾渴的日子裡，她要到哪裡注滿她的水罐啊？」我們沮喪的問著彼此，「在我們生活的這些山的外面，還有土地嗎？」

　　那是一個夏天的夜晚，微風從南方吹來，我坐在她的荒廢的房子裡，那盞熄滅的燈，仍然一動也不動的站在那裡。就在那個時候，忽然之間，群山在我的眼前消失了，就像窗簾被拉開一樣。「啊，那來的，不正是她嗎！你好嗎，我的孩子？你幸福嗎？但是，你在這個毫無遮攔的天空下，要在哪裡安身呢？還有，天啊，我們的清泉不在這裡，不能舒緩你的乾渴。」

　　「那裡還是同一片天空，」她說，「只是沒有群山的環繞——還是同一股清泉，流成江河——還是同一片土地，擴展成平原。」

　　「真是樣樣齊全，」我嘆道，「只是沒有我們。」她悲傷的笑了笑，說：「你們在我的心裡。」我醒來了，在夜色中，聽著泉水潺潺，聽著雪松沙沙作響。

In the month of May the sun grew strong and the snow melted, and we sat by the spring and wept. We wondered in our mind, "Is there a spring in the land where she has gone and where she can fill her vessel in these hot thirsty days?" And we asked each other in dismay, "Is there a land beyond these hills where we live?"

It was a summer night; the breeze blew from the south; and I sat in her deserted room where the lamp stood still unlit. When suddenly from before my eyes the hills vanished like curtains drawn aside. "Ah, it is she who comes. How are you, my child? Are you happy? But where can you shelter under this open sky? And, alas, our spring is not here to allay your thirst."

"Here is the same sky," she said, "only free from the fencing hills, —— this is the same stream grown into a river, —— the same earth widened into a plain."

"Everything is here," I sighed, "only we are not." She smiled sadly and said, "You are in my heart." I woke up and heard the babbling of the stream and the rustling of the deodars at night.

　　黃綠相間的稻田上，掠過秋日的雲影，後面緊跟著狂追的太陽。

　　蜜蜂忘記吸吮花蜜，它們愚笨的盤旋著，嗡嗡的唱著，陶醉於光明中。

　　鴨子們在河中的小島上，無緣無故的歡快的喧鬧著。

　　誰都不要回家吧，兄弟們，今天早上，誰都不要去工作。

　　讓我們用狂風暴雨佔領藍天，讓我們飛奔著搶奪空間。

　　笑聲在空氣裡遊蕩，像洪水上的泡沫。

　　兄弟們，讓我們在空虛無聊的歌聲中，揮霍我們的清晨吧！

EIGHTY-FOUR

Over the green and yellow rice-fields sweep the shadows of the autumn clouds followed by the swift-chasing sun.

The bees forget to sip their honey; drunken with light they foolishly hover and hum.

The ducks in the islands of the river clamour in joy for mere nothing.

Let none go back home, brothers, this morning, let none go to work.

Let us take the blue sky by storm and plunder space as we run.

Laughter floats in the air like foam on the flood.

Brothers, let us squander our morning in futile songs.

你是誰，讀者，百年之後，讀著我的詩？

我無法從春天的財富裡為你送去一朵鮮花，從遠方的雲彩裡為你送去一縷金霞。

打開你的門，向四周看看。

從你的繁花盛開的花園中，採集百年之前消失的鮮花的芬芳記憶。

在你的內心的歡樂裡，願你感受吟唱春日清晨的鮮活喜悅，讓歡快的聲音穿越一百年的時光。

EIGHTY-FIVE

Who are you, reader, reading my poems an hundred years hence?

I cannot send you one single flower from this wealth of the spring, one single streak of gold from yonder clouds.

Open your doors and look abroad.

From your blossoming garden gather fragrant memories of the vanished flowers of an hundred years before.

In the joy of your heart may you feel the living joy that sang one spring morning, sending its glad voice across an hundred years.

海鴿文化出版圖書有限公司
Seadove Publishing Company Ltd.,

作者　　　　羅賓德拉納德·泰戈爾
譯者　　　　徐翰林
美術構成　　驟賴耙工作室
封面設計　　斐類設計工作室
發行人　　　羅清維
企畫執行　　林義傑、張緯倫
責任行政　　陳淑貞

出版　　　　海鴿文化出版圖書有限公司
出版登記　　行政院新聞局局版北市業字第780號
發行部　　　台北市信義區林口街54-4號1樓
電話　　　　02-27273008
傳真　　　　02-27270603
網址　　　　www.seadove.com.tw
e - mail　　service@seadove.com.tw

總經銷　　　創智文化有限公司
住址　　　　台北縣中和市建一路136號5樓
電話　　　　02-22289828
傳真　　　　02-22287858

香港總經銷　時代文化有限公司
住址　　　　香港九龍旺角塘尾道64號
　　　　　　龍駒企業大廈7樓A室
電話　　　　(852)3165-1105
傳真　　　　(852)2381-9888

出版日期　　2010年01月01日　一版一刷
定價　　　　169元
郵政劃撥　　18989626 戶名：海鴿文化出版圖書有限公司

園丁集／羅賓德拉納德·泰戈爾 著；徐翰林 譯 一 一
版，臺北市 ： 海鴿文化，2009.12
面 ； 公分.－－（青春講義；92）
譯自 ： The gardener
ISBN 978-986-6340-12-3（平裝）

867.51　　　　　　　　　　　　　　　98020487

Seadove

Seadove